HYPNOTIZING
MARIA

Also by Richard Bach

RICHARD BACH

Bestselling author of *Jonathan Livingston Seagull* and *Illusions*

HYPNOTIZING
MARIA

A STORY

HAMPTON ROADS
PUBLISHING COMPANY, INC.

Hypnotizing Maria
A Story

Richard Bach

Cover design by Frame25 Productions
Cover art by John Rawsterne, Johan Swanepoel, and Vibrant Image
Studio c/o Shutterstock.com, and Richard Bach

"The Trucker's Code" is from the novel, *The Box*, by Jay (O. J.) Bryson
(www.thetruckerscode.com). Reprinted by permission of the author.

Hampton Roads Publishing Company, Inc.
PO Box 8107
Charlottesville, VA 22906

434-296-2772 • fax: 434-296-5096
e-mail: hrpc@hrpub.com • www.hrpub.com

If you are unable to order this book from your local
bookseller, you may order directly from the publisher.
Call 434-296-2772.

Library of Congress Cataloging-in-Publication Data

Bach, Richard.
  Hypnotizing Maria : a novel./ Richard Bach.
    p. cm.
  Summary: "An exploration of deep spiritual and philosophical
issues through the eyes of a pilot"--Provided by publisher.
  ISBN 978-1-57174-623-8 (alk. paper)
  1. Air pilots--Fiction. I. Title.
PS3552.A255H96 2009
813'.54--dc22
                                                    2009012402

ISBN 978-1-57174-623-8
10 9 8 7 6 5 4 3 2 1
Printed on acid-free paper in the United States

CHAPTER ONE

J amie Forbes flew airplanes. That's all he'd done that mattered since he dropped out of college, back when, and got his pilot's license. If it had wings, he loved it.

He flew fighters in the Air Force, didn't much care for the politics and the additional duties and the odd lack of flying time. He chose to leave early, when the service offered it.

The airlines wouldn't have him. He applied one time and the questions on the pilot exam weeded him out.

"1. If you had to choose, would you be a tree or a stone?

"2. Which color is better, red or blue?"

He didn't answer these, as they had nothing to do with flying.

"3. Are details important?"

"Of course they're not important," he said. "What's important is arriving safely on the ground, every time. Who cares if you shine your shoes?"

Wrong answer, he found, when the examiner looked him in the eye and said, "We do."

But there's plenty to be done in aviation besides flying fighter planes and jet transports. There's charter and corporate flying and the scenic-ride business; there's crop dusting and air show aerobatics and pipeline patrol and aerial photography; there's aircraft ferrying to be done; there's banner towing, glider towing, carting skydivers up and turning them loose in the sky; there's air racing, television news flying, traffic reporting, police flying, flight testing, freight dogging and barnstorming old biplanes out of hayfields. And teaching, of course, always new folks coming along with the same destiny to fly as his own . . . there's always flight instructing.

He'd done it all as his life went by. These last years he had become a flight instructor and a good one, according to the adage that you tell the best instructors by the color of their hair.

Not that he was some old-timer, mind you, or that he had nothing left to learn. He'd just packed his share of flying into those decades since solo, coming up on twelve thousand flying hours. Not a whole lot of time, not a little. Enough that Jamie Forbes had learned humility.

Inside, though, he was still the kid wild to fly anything he could get his little paws on.

That's all as it should be, and nobody's interest, save for what happened last September. What happened then won't matter to some; to others it'll change their lives the way it did mine.

CHAPTER TWO

At the time, he thought it was coincidence. Jamie Forbes was flying his Beech T-34 from Washington State to Florida, turning winter to summer in his flight-training business by pointing the nose southeast for sixteen flying hours, four hours at a time.

The '34, if you're not familiar with it, is the first airplane the Air Force trusted to an aviation cadet, years ago: a single engine, low wing, two-place tandem propeller-driven machine, 225 horsepower. Cockpit like a fighter plane's, so the transition from trainer to fighter would be easy for new pilots.

He never imagined then, marching and studying, memorizing checklists and Morse code and the rules of aerodynamics, that years later he'd own the same airplane himself, considerably spiffed up the way civilians do when they get their hands on a surplus military machine.

His T-34 today had the 300-horsepower Continental engine, for instance, a three-blade propeller, an instrument panel with navigation equipment that hadn't been invented when the airplane was new, sky-blue military camouflage, restored Air Force markings. It's a well-designed aircraft and a dear little machine to fly.

He flew alone, from Seattle in the morning to Twin Falls, Idaho. Takeoff at noon from Twin Falls over Ogden and Rock Springs, toward North Platte, Nebraska.

It happened an hour out of North Platte, twenty minutes north of Cheyenne.

"I think he's dead!"

A woman's voice on the radio. "Can anybody hear me? *I think my husband died!"*

She was transmitting on 122.8 megacycles, the small-airport unicom frequency, her voice loud and clear—she couldn't have been too far away.

Nobody answered.

"You can do this, Mister Forbes." Calm and patient, touch of the South in that unforgettable voice.

"Mister Dexter?" he said it aloud, thunderstruck. His flying instructor from forty years past, a voice he'd never forget. He shot a glance to the mirror, checking the rear cockpit. It was empty, of course.

Not another sound but the engine rumbling loud and smooth ahead.

"Somebody God help me he's died!"

He pressed the microphone button.

"Maybe so, ma'am," said Jamie Forbes, "but maybe not. You can fly the airplane without him."

"No I never learned! Juan's over against the door, he's not moving!"

"We'd better get him on the ground," he said, choosing "we" because of what he figured she'd say next.

"I can't fly an airplane!"

"OK," he said, "then you and I'll get him down together."

It happens once in practically never, a passenger at the controls when a pilot's incapacitated. Lucky for them all, it was a pretty day for flying.

"You know how the controls work, ma'am?" he asked. "You move the steering wheel, keep the wings level?"

"Yes." That made it easy.

"Just keep the wings level, for now." He asked her when and where they had taken off and where they were headed, he turned due east and sure enough, a minute later he could see a Cessna 182 at ten o'clock low, just forward of the T-34's left wing.

"Give us just a bit of a right turn," he said. "We've got you in sight."

If the airplane didn't turn, he didn't have her in sight at all, but he gambled and won. The wings tilted.

He dropped down inside her turn and came alongside, sliding into formation fifty feet away.

"If you look over to your right . . ." he said.

She looked and he waved to her.

"Everything's going to be OK now," he said. "Let's get you over to the airport and land."

"I don't know how to fly!" She said that and the wings banked more steeply, toward him.

He banked with her, two airplanes turning together. "That'll be no problem, ma'am," he said, "I'm an instructor."

"Thank God," she said, her airplane falling into a steeper bank.

"You might turn that wheel to the left," he said. "Not a whole lot, just firm and gentle to the left. That'll bring you back to level flight."

She looked ahead, turned the wheel, and the Cessna's wings rolled level.

"You've got it," he said. "You sure you've never flown before?"

Her voice came a little calmer. "I've watched Juan fly."

"Well, you watched real good." He found she knew where the throttle was, the rudder pedals, got her to turn her airplane to the left till she was headed back toward the airport at Cheyenne.

"What's your name, ma'am?"

"I'm scared," she said. *"I can't do this!"*

"Don't you be kidding me. You've been flying this airplane five minutes already and you're doing a great job. Just relax, take it easy, pretend you're an airline captain."

"Pretend I'm what?" She heard, couldn't believe what this person was saying.

"Forget everything but you're the airline captain, you're the first woman captain the company's ever hired and you've been flying for years and years. You're completely comfortable in the airplane, happy as can be.

Landing a little Cessna on a beautiful day like this? Piece of cake!"

This man is out of his mind, she thought, but he's an instructor. "Piece of cake," she said.

"Right you are. What's your favorite cake?"

She looked at him out the right window of the Cessna, a stricken uncomprehending smile, some of her fear melting in I'm-going-to-die and he's asking me about *cake?* Of all rescuers I get a *crazy-man?*

"Carrot?" she said.

He smiled back. Good. She knows I'm nuts, now she's got to be the sane one and that means staying calm. "Piece of carrot cake."

"My name's Maria." As though knowing that might put him in his right mind.

Cheyenne airport appeared, a streak on the horizon. Fifteen miles out, seven minutes flying. He chose Cheyenne for its long runways and ambulance, instead of landing at the small airports closer.

"Why don't you try pushing that throttle in, Maria? You'll hear the engine; it'll get louder, as you know, and the airplane will start to climb, just gently. Push it all the way in, now, and we'll practice a little climb, here."

He wanted to remind her of the climb, of course, in case she got too low on her landing approach. He wanted her to know she was safe in the sky and pushing the throttle is the way to get back up when she wants to.

"You're doin' fine, Captain," he said. "You're a natural pilot."

Then he had her pull the throttle back, ease the nose just below the horizon, and they descended together down to traffic pattern altitude.

The lady alongside looked back at him from her airplane.

Two machines nearly touching in the air, yet nothing he could do would fly her airplane for her. All he had was words.

"Almost home," he told her. "Maria, you're doing a mighty fine piece of flying. Just turn toward me a bit, for about ten seconds or so, then roll back level."

She pressed the microphone button but didn't say anything. The airplane banked to the right.

"You're doin' fine. I'm going to talk to the control tower on another radio. Don't worry, I'll be listening on this radio, too. You can talk to me any time you want, OK?"

She nodded.

He switched the number two com radio to Cheyenne's frequency, called the control tower. "Hi

Cheyenne, this is Cessna 2461 Echo." The aircraft number was painted on the side of her airplane. No need to give them his own.

"Six One Echo, go ahead."

"Six One Echo's a flight of two, eight miles north for landing."

"Roger Six One Echo. Call entering the left downwind for Runway Niner."

"Wilco," he said. Funny word: it means *I will comply*. "And Six One Echo's a Cessna 182, pilot's incapacitated. The passenger's flying the airplane, I'm flying alongside, helping her out."

There was a silence. "Say again, Six One Echo? The pilot's what?"

"Pilot's unconscious. Passenger's flying the airplane."

"Roger. You're cleared to land any runway. Are you declaring an emergency?"

"Negative. We'll take Runway Niner. She's doing fine, but it wouldn't hurt to roll an ambulance for the pilot, and a fire truck. Keep the vehicles behind the landing aircraft, will you? We don't want to distract her, equipment driving alongside when she's touching down."

"Roger, we'll roll the equipment and keep it behind the aircraft. Break: All aircraft in the Cheyenne area depart the airport traffic pattern please, we have an emergency in progress."

"She's on unicom, Tower, two-two-eight. I'll be talking to her that frequency but listening yours."

"Roger, Six One Echo. Good luck."

"Not required. She's doing fine."

He switched the transmitter back to unicom.

"There's the airport way out to your left, Maria," he said. "We're going to do a big gentle turn to line up with the runway. Real smooth, no hurry. This is easy for you."

They flew a huge landing pattern, mild slow turns, the instructor talking her through.

"Right about here, you can ease the throttle back, let the nose come down just below the horizon like we did before, a nice easy descent. The airplane loves this."

She nodded. If this man is chattering away about airplanes loving things, then it probably isn't all that dangerous, what we're doing.

"If we don't like this approach," he said, "we can climb up and do approaches all day long, if we want. This one's lookin' just fine, though. You're doin' great." He didn't ask how much fuel she had remaining.

The two aircraft gentled left onto final approach, the runway lining up ahead, wide concrete two miles long.

"What we're gonna do is touch down real smooth, we're gonna put one wheel on each side of that big white line down the center of the runway. Lookin' good, Captain. Add just a little power, throttle forward about half an inch . . ."

She was responding well, now, and calm.

"Bring that throttle back just a bit. You are a fantastic pilot, by the way. You're smooth on the controls . . ."

He moved a few feet farther from her wing as the airplanes sank earthward.

"Just hold what you have, fly it straight down that centerline . . . there you go, very nice. Relax, relax . . . wiggle your toes. You're flyin' like an old-timer. Ease the throttle back now an inch . . . Ease the control wheel back 'bout three inches, now. It'll feel a little heavy and that's just how it should feel. Lookin' beautiful, you are gonna make a fantastic landing."

The wheels were four feet above the runway . . . three feet.

"Hold that nose up just where you have it, now just ease the throttle all the way back, all the way."

The wheels touched the runway, puffs of blue rubber-smoke from the tires.

"Perfect touchdown," he said, "perfect landing. You can let go of the control wheel now, you don't need it on the ground. Steer the airplane straight with the foot pedals and let it roll to a stop, right there on the runway. Ambulance'll be alongside right quick."

He pushed his own throttle and the T-34 swept past her airplane, climbing.

"Nice landing," he said. "You're an awfully good pilot."

She didn't reply.

He watched down over his shoulder as the ambulance sped onto the runway behind her. It slowed as her airplane slowed, then stopped, doors flying open. The fire truck, red and square, trundled along behind, unneeded.

As the control tower had enough to keep it busy, he said nothing more. In less than a minute his airplane was out of sight toward North Platte.

CHAPTER THREE

The story from the newspaper was pinned on the bulletin board at North Platte Lee Bird airport next morning: *Pilot Stricken, Wife Lands Plane.*

Jamie Forbes frowned at that. "Wife" equals "non-pilot." It's going to take a while, he thought, for folks to understand there's lots of women out there licensed pilots, and more every day.

After the headline, though, the reporter told the story fairly straight. When her husband collapsed in the air, Maria Ochoa, 63, thought he had died; she was frightened, called for help, et cetera.

Then he read this: "I never could've landed by myself, but the man in the other plane said I could. I swear to God he hypnotized me, right in the air. 'Pretend you're an airline pilot.' I pretended because I don't know how to fly. But when I woke up, the airplane had landed safe!"

The story said her husband had suffered a stroke and would recover.

Airline-captain role play works well for students, he thought, it always has.

He stumbled, though, on what she had said.

Hypnotized her? He walked to the airport café for breakfast, wondering hypnotism, remembering thirty years gone as though it had been yesterday.

CHAPTER FOUR

He had taken a seat in an aisle up front, row A, expecting when Blacksmyth the Great called for volunteers from the audience, he might be asked.

Near the end of the show, it felt like fun to step up to the stage, though he doubted he could be hypnotized and wouldn't be chosen. Two others, man and woman, joined him there.

Blacksmyth the hypnotist, distinguished in white tie and tuxedo but friendly of voice and manner, asked the three to stand in a row and they did, facing the audience. Jamie Forbes was on the end closest to stage center.

The showman stepped behind the volunteers, touched the woman on the shoulder, pulling her gently off balance. She took a step back to regain it.

He did the same to the next in line, and the man stepped back, as well.

Forbes resolved to be different. When the hypnotist's hand touched his shoulder, he tilted with the pressure, trusting that the man wouldn't have much of a show if he let his subject fall over on stage.

Blacksmyth caught him at once, thanked the other volunteers and dismissed them to a round of applause.

Things had gone too far. "I'm sorry," Jamie whispered while the sounds died away, "but I can't be hypnotized."

"Oh," replied the performer, softly. "Then what are you doing on this planet?"

The hypnotist paused, saying nothing, and began to smile at Jamie Forbes. A murmur of laughter from audience—what was going to happen to this poor subject?

Just now the subject felt sorry for the entertainer, thought better of walking off-stage, and decided that he might as well play along. He had warned the man, but there was no cause to embarrass him in front of a thousand paying customers.

"What is your name, sir?" the hypnotist asked, loud enough for all to hear.

"Jamie."

"Jamie, have we met?" he asked. "Have we ever seen each other before this evening?"

"No sir, we have not."

"That is correct. Now Jamie," he said, "let's you and me take a little walk in our minds. You see these seven steps ahead of us, we'll go down the steps together. Together we'll go down the steps; down, down, deeper, deeper . . ."

Jamie Forbes didn't notice the steps at first. They must have been plastic or balsa wood, painted to look like stone, and he walked them down with the hypnotist, step by step. He wondered how the audience could see the show when the volunteer was going to wind up practically underneath the stage, but concluded that was Blacksmyth's problem. He must have some scheme with mirrors.

At the bottom of the steps was a heavy wooden door. Blacksmyth asked him to step through, and when he did, closed the door behind him. His voice came clearly through the walls, describing for the audience what Jamie saw before him: an empty stone room, no doors, no windows, yet plenty of light.

The room wasn't square but round, and when he turned to see where he entered, the door had disappeared. Disguised, probably, to match the stone.

Seems like stone, he reminded myself. Painted cloth to look like irregular squares of granite, some medieval fortress.

"Look around you, Jamie," said Blacksmyth from outside, "and tell us what you see."

He chose not to say what he knew, that it was cloth. "Looks like a stone room," he said, "inside a castle tower. No windows. No doors."

"Are you sure it's stone?" came the hypnotist's voice.

Don't push me, he thought. Don't count on me to lie for you. "Looks like stone. I'm not sure."

"Find out."

It's your reputation, Mr. Blacksmyth, he thought. He walked to the wall, touched it. It felt rough and hard. He pushed, gently. "It feels like stone."

"I want you to be sure, Jamie. Put your hands on the stone and push as hard as you can. The harder you push, the more solid it will become."

What an odd thing to say. As hard as I can push is pretty hard, he thought, and there's going to be wood blocks all over your stage. He pushed gently, at first, then harder, then harder still. It was solid, all right. This may be more a magic show, he thought, than mind stuff. How did Blacksmyth build a stone room under the stage, and how does he move it from theater to theater?

He looked for the door behind its disguise, but everywhere was stone. He pressed against the wall, kicked it here and there, walked around a room no more than ten feet in diameter, straining against the granite, kicking it hard enough to dent, if it were balsa wood or plastic.

It was frightening but not much, as he knew Blacksmyth would have to set him free some time soon.

"Jamie, there's a way out," said the showman. "Can you tell us what it is?"

I could climb it, he thought, if the spaces between the stones were wider. Looking upward, he saw a ceiling of the same stuff, solid blocks. On one part of the wall was a scorched blackened place, as though there had been a torch placed there for light. Now the torch and the fitting that held it were gone.

"I can't climb it," he said.

"You say you cannot climb the wall," said Blacksmyth, loud and theatrical. "Jamie, have you tried?"

He took that for a hint, that there may be hidden handholds.

Not. He stepped on the edge of the first course of stone, his shoe slipped off at once.

"There's no climbing it," he said.

"Can you tunnel *under* the wall, Jamie?"

That seemed like a silly idea, the floor being the same stuff as the wall and ceiling. He knelt down and scratched at the surface, but it was as unyielding as the rest of the room.

"How about the door? Try the door."

"Door's gone," he replied, feeling foolish. How could the door be gone? He knew it was part of the trick, but the fact was that a door no longer existed.

Crossing to where he entered, Jamie Forbes threw his shoulder against what looked like stone but may have been stuccoed plywood. He tried that, succeeded in bruising his shoulder. How did the whole place get to be rock?

"There's a way out," said Blacksmyth again. "Can you tell us what it is?"

Jamie Forbes was tired and frustrated. Whatever was going on, the trick was getting old. No doors, no windows, no keys, no ropes or wires or pulleys, no tools, no known combination of touching this slab then that one. If there were a way out, some secret password that needed shouting, he hadn't a clue.

"Give up?"

Instead of answering, he backed against one side of the room, ran three steps and gave a flying kick to the other. He wound up on the ground, of course, the wall unmarked.

"Yeah," he said, getting up again. "I give."

"Here's the answer," came Blacksmyth's voice, filled with drama. "Jamie, *walk through the wall!*"

The man's gone mad, he thought, he's lost it in the middle of his show. "I can't do that," he said, a little sullen. "I don't walk through walls."

"Jamie, I'm going to tell you the truth. I am not kidding. The walls are in your mind. You can walk through them if you believe you can."

He rested his hand, at arm's length, on the stone. "Yeah," he said, "right."

"OK, Jamie. I'll give it all away for you, right now; I'll give the whole trick away. You don't recall this, but you've been hypnotized. There are no walls around you. You are standing on a stage in the Lafayette Hotel in Long Beach, California, and you are the only person in this hall who believes that you've been walled in."

The stone didn't flicker. "Why are you doing this to me," he asked. "Are you doing this for fun?"

"Yes, Jamie," said Blacksmyth gently. "We are doing this for fun. You volunteered for this and for so long as you live, you shall never forget what is happening today."

"Help me, please," he said, not a trace of pride or anger.

"I'll help you help yourself," said Blacksmyth. "We need never be prisoner of our own beliefs. At the count of three, I shall walk through the stone at one side of the room. I shall take your hand in mine and we shall walk together through the wall on the other side. And you will be free."

What does one say to that? Jamie chose silence.

"One," came the hypnotist's voice. "Two. . . ." Long pause. "Three."

All at once, it was as Blacksmyth had said. For an instant, Jamie caught a blurry twisted place in the stone, as though it were dry water; the next instant Blacksmyth in his spotless tuxedo stepped through the wall into the prison, offering his hand.

Flooded with relief, Jamie took the man's hand. "I didn't think . . ."

The hypnotist neither slowed nor replied, striding toward the stone on the opposite side of the room, pulling his subject with him.

It must have sounded like a scream, though he didn't mean it that way. From Jamie Forbes came a cry of fearsome baffled astonishment.

Blacksmyth's body disappeared into the stone. For an instant Jamie held tightly to a disembodied arm, whose wrist and hand moved forward, drawing him directly into the wall.

Whatever next sound he gave might have been muffled by the wall, and in the following instant there was a click like the snap of fingers and he stood back on stage, holding Mr. Blacksmyth's hand, blinking in the spotlight, enveloped in fascinated applause.

The people he could see, in the first rows before the dark behind the spotlights, were rising to their feet, a standing ovation for the hypnotist, and in an odd way, for himself.

The act was Blacksmyth's finale. He left his subject soaked in applause, disappeared into the wings, returned twice to the stage before the sound of the crowd hushed to gentle patter and the murmur of many voices, folks gathering their programs, jackets and purses as the house lights came up.

Jamie Forbes made his way unsteadily down the steps to the main floor, a few of the audience there to smile and thank him for his courage to volunteer: "Was it real, did it feel real to you, the stone and all?"

"Of course it was real!"

They laughed, then puzzled smiles, explaining. "You were on the stage, in the center. Empty stage! Blacksmyth on the left, talking to you. You made it seem so real! The leap at the end, and the kick, it was amazing! You really believed . . . did you?"

More than believed. He knew.

Jamie Forbes lived the evening through, over and again, all the way back to his apartment.

Stone solid as any boulder, hard as any steel that ever he had touched. Belief? He would have starved to death in that room, trapped there by . . . by what? More than belief. By absolute, unquestioning conviction.

From the barest of suggestions: "Let's you and me take a little walk in our minds . . ."

What was I thinking, "I can't be hypnotized?" I fell for some smooth talk, I was convinced into prison. How can that happen?

Years later, he learned he wouldn't have died there, left alone. He would finally have slept, and waking, recovered from the prison-beliefs that seemed so real to him a few hours before.

CHAPTER FIVE

The sign in the lobby next evening was unchanged:

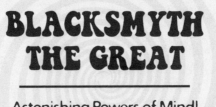

BLACKSMYTH THE GREAT

Astonishing Powers of Mind!
ON STAGE TONIGHT!

This last night of the show, Jamie Forbes took a seat mid-audience, row S center, a hundred feet from the stage. No volunteering this time, he thought. Tonight we watch. What did this man do to me? How did he do it?

Each act was fun, of course, but he shrugged the fun aside and watched what happened: a few quiet words and the first volunteer was lost in trance.

One glance through a shuffled deck, she could recall the sequence of fifty-two playing cards, error-free, as they were drawn from the deck.

"Your arm is as stiff and solid as an iron bar," commanded the hypnotist to a relatively small volunteer, and no man from the audience was strong enough to bend it.

"You can clearly see the spirit of Mrs. Dora Chapman's departed husband," he suggested to a teenage girl, "standing before you now. Can you describe Mister Chapman for us?"

"Yes, sir," she said, unblinking. "He's tall, slender, brown eyes, black hair combed straight back, a small mustache. He smiles as though he is awfully happy. He is wearing what look like riding clothes, formal and . . . dashing, I guess you'd call it, a black bow tie . . ."

After her description his photograph flashed onscreen for the audience to see, the man in different clothes, but as she said. A sling supported his arm, sprained or broken not long before the photo was taken, but it was the man, all right. Somehow she saw him, unless the girl was cheating, already clued about the subject, which Jamie Forbes doubted.

"He loved riding, and his horse . . . ," his widow whispered to Blacksmyth, then repeated it, a soft voice in the microphone, when he asked her to tell the audience.

So it went, as Blacksmyth delivered on his promise, astonishing powers brought forth, from people as ordinary as Jamie himself had been the evening before.

Is this audience, he wondered, all past-show volunteers, trying to understand what happened to us last week?

It was all he could do to keep from reliving his own trance, came the show's final act. There the three volunteers on stage. One stepped back as the hypnotist pressed gently on a shoulder, the second began to fall and was caught at once, the third resisted the touch. First and third excused with thanks and applause, courtesy somehow important to the showman.

Jamie strained to catch Blacksmyth's words, softly spoken to the remaining volunteer, tried to read his lips. All he caught was the word "voyage." The hypnotist said something different to her than he had to Jamie the night before, took a few more seconds with her.

"And what is your name, ma'am?" he asked for all to hear.

"Lonnie," she replied, a firm voice.

"That is correct!" he said. Waiting for the laughter to die, he raised his voice, continued. "Now Lonnie, have you and I ever met, have we ever seen each other before this evening?"

"No."

"That is true," he said. "Lonnie, if you will kindly step this way . . ."

Nothing could Jamie Forbes see that pointed an arrow: "Hypnotist," toward the man on stage; no label for her: "Already in Trance." Just two people walking slowly together, an everyday moment.

They moved from the edge of the stage to the center. She continued three steps farther by herself, as though unaware she was alone, turned, and began to look about her.

Jamie's hands went cold. He knew what she was seeing: walls, stone, the prison cell. But there was nothing around her. Nothing. Air. Stage. Audience. Not the sheerest curtain, no mirrors, no tricks of lighting.

Yet her face clouded, as he knew his had. What had become of the door? Where had Blacksmyth gone?

It hadn't occurred to him: where was the light coming from? Nor did it occur to her. He wondered if she saw the burnt torch-mark on the stone.

He watched her reach to the invisible wall, touch it. Push against it, move left, push again.

She may be imagining a different sort of stone, he thought, but she had created it just as hard, just as solid.

"Hello . . ." she said. "Can anybody hear me?"

The audience chuckled, of course we can hear you. We're right here!

Jamie Forbes didn't smile. About now, he had been a little frightened.

Frightened of what? Why had he been afraid?

Trapped, that's why. Locked in stone. No doors, no windows, stone ceiling stone floor . . . bug in a teacup, no way out.

All of it wrong, he thought, watching. Blacksmyth had said to walk down the steps, had murmured something more. At the bottom of the steps was the door. Every minute as real as yesterday. Tonight he saw it differently—the stage, an empty stage with that poor woman walled by her own mind.

The audience smiled, fascinated, while it was all Jamie could do to keep himself in the seat, stop himself from bolting down the aisle to the stage, rescue her, save her . . .

From what, Jamie, he thought, save her from what? How do you unhypnotize someone sunk deep in knowing that massive walls which you cannot see are pressing in on her, imprisoning her, no food no water, air itself running out?

Who could have reached him, told him his walls were fantasy and made him believe it?

I wouldn't have seen rescuers, he thought. Not until they were close enough.

Close enough and then what? I'd see someone walking to me out of solid stone, this is a person I'm suddenly going to believe? He'll say it's all in your mind and I'm going to say oh, sure, thank you and my walls will disappear?

"Hello?" said Lonnie. "Mister Blacksmyth? Did you mean to leave me here? Mister Blacksmyth can you hear me? Mister Blacksmyth!"

Jamie looked at the hypnotist. How can he stand it, her screams? because in a minute she'll be screaming.

Lonnie threw herself against the curving stone of her mind, pounded on it so that her fists would bleed, before long.

Enough, Blacksmyth, he thought. There's enough, now.

A hush of whispers began in the auditorium, smiles gone, audience getting uncomfortable.

Perfect timing, the hypnotist walked to stand not five feet from his subject, every eye in the house upon him.

"Lonnie, there's a way out," he said. "Can you tell us what it is?"

Her face was anguished now. "No," she said, hopeless.

For God's sake, Lonnie, thought Jamie Forbes, walk over and punch the guy!

It would be years before he learned that Blacksmyth was to her what hypnotists call a negative hallucination—she couldn't see him, blocked as he was by the positive hallucination of the stone she saw close by, locking her in.

In that moment Jamie Forbes thought that nothing in the world could wake her but the snap of Blacksmyth's fingers, no matter she was starving, or dying of thirst. Not true, but that's what he believed, watching.

"Have you tried," said Blacksmyth, "every possible way, to get out?"

She nodded, head down, both hands pushing against the stone of her belief.

"Give up?"

She nodded, pitiful, exhausted.

"Here's the answer," came his voice, filled with drama. "Lonnie, *walk through the wall!*"

She did nothing. Already she was pushing against the stone, leaning in an odd posture that seemed impossible to hold, pushing against empty air.

How could she walk through, how could her body go where her hands could not?

"Lonnie, I'm going to tell you the truth. I'm not kidding. The wall is in your mind. You can walk through it if only you believe you can."

How many times had Blacksmyth said those words? What does it do to your heart, telling the truth to someone incapable of believing it?

"I'll give it all away for you, Lonnie, right now." He turned and spoke this drama to the audience. "You've been hypnotized. There are no walls around you. You are standing on a stage in the Lafayette Hotel in Long Beach, California, and you are the only person in this hall who believes that you're locked in that prison."

"Please don't hurt me," she said.

"I will not hurt you, I promise. I will help you help yourself," he said. "We need never be prisoner of our own beliefs. We can remember who we are. At the count of Three I shall walk through the wall at one side of the room, I shall take your hand in mine and we shall walk together through the other side. And you will be free."

Lonnie coughed a short hopeless laugh. *Just let me out.*

"One," said Blacksmyth. "Two."

"Three."

The hypnotist did what anyone in the audience could have done. He took four steps and stood beside her.

Lonnie gasped and screamed at the sight of him, freezing blood to ice.

Blacksmyth offered his hand, but she threw her arms around him, clinging to her rescuer.

"Together now," he said. He took her wrist. "We'll walk together through . . ."

"NO!" she screamed. *"NO! NO!"*

"We'll use the door," he said, calm and even.

This had happened before, Jamie knew it at once. Lonnie had gone far enough over the edge that the hypnotist moved to Plan B: Suggest the Door.

What was Plan C, he wondered. That would be a snap of the fingers, wake her now into the world of the stage, the audience; she had volunteered . . .

She shook free, desperate relief, grabbed the invisible handle to an invisible door, ran a few steps and halted, breathing hard, turning to the hypnotist. He reached for her hand and this time she took it. He raised his other hand by his cheek, smiling into her eyes, and snapped his fingers.

It was as though he had slapped her face. She jolted back, eyes wide.

Next second came a shock-wave of applause, shattering unbearable tension in the hall, some folks standing already, transfixed by what had happened before their eyes.

Blacksmyth bowed, and as he was holding her hand, she bowed also, bewildered.

The roar filled the hall, astonished wonder.

In the midst of it, Lonnie brushed her tears, and even from row S, Jamie Forbes read her distress: *What did you do to me?*

Blacksmyth answered a few words only she could hear, turned, and mouthed thank-you to the applause, his expression: *Don't underestimate the force of your own belief!*

Jamie Forbes was lost in the strange demonstration for days after, turned it this way and that in his mind till it washed away without answer, fading before his life-long obsession with flying.

He buried that mystery till a long time later, till well after first light of a day in North Platte, Nebraska.

CHAPTER SIX

Eight-thirty in the morning, the airport café was crowded. He found a place for himself, opened a menu.

"Mind if I share your table?"

Jamie Forbes looked up at her, one of those folks you like the minute you meet. "Share away," he said.

She set a backpack alongside. "Is this where I learn how to fly?"

"Nope," he said, pointed out the window at the sky. "You learn to fly up there."

She looked, and nodded. "Always said some day I'd get to it. Learn to fly. I promised myself; didn't quite make it come true."

"It's never too late," he said.

"Oh . . ." she said, a wistful smile. "I think it is for me." She extended her hand. "Dee Hallock."

"Jamie Forbes."

They looked at the menu. Something light, just a bit, he thought. Orange juice and toast would be healthy.

"You're traveling," he said.

"Yes. Hitchhiking." She put the menu down, and when the waitress arrived, she said, "Tea and toast, please. Mint and wheat."

"Yes, ma'am," said the waitress, memorizing an easy one, and turned to him.

"Hot chocolate and rye toast, if I could." Hitchhiking?

"You're flying today," said the waitress. "All these light orders, this morning."

"Light is good," he said. She smiled and left to another table, their orders in her mind.

"Are you hitchhiking cars," he asked, "or airplanes?"

"I hadn't thought of airplanes," said Dee. "Can one do that?"

"Never hurts to ask. You want to be careful, though."

"Oh?"

"This is high country. Some airplanes don't fly as well as others, up high, with passengers." Early forties, he thought. Businesswoman. What's she doing hitch-hiking?

"To answer your question," she said, "I'm testing an hypothesis." Dark brown hair, brown eyes, that magnetic beauty that curiosity and intelligence bring to a woman's face.

"My question?"

"'How come she's hitchhiking?'"

He blinked. "You're right. I was thinking something like that. What's your hypothesis?"

"There's no coincidence."

Interesting, he thought. "What kind of coincidence, there isn't?"

"I'm an equal-opportunity explorer," she said. "What kind doesn't matter. You and I, for instance; I wouldn't be surprised if both of us knew some important mutual friend. Wouldn't be surprised there's a reason we're meeting. Not at all." She looked at him as though she knew there was.

"Of course there's no way to tell," he said.

She smiled. "Except by coincidence."

"Which there's no such thing as."

"That's what I'm finding out."

Nice quest, he thought. "And you're finding more coincidences per mile on the road than you do in your office?"

She nodded.

"You don't find it dangerous, hitchhiking? An attractive woman asking to be picked up by anybody on the road?"

A that's-impossible laugh. "I don't attract danger."

I'll bet, he thought. Are you so sure of yourself, or are you just naïve? "How's your hypothesis holding up?"

"I'm not ready to call it a law, but I think it'll be my theory, at least, before long."

She had smiled about attracting danger—he wouldn't understand that yet.

"Am I a coincidence?" he asked.

"Is Jamie a coincidence?" She said it as though she were asking someone he couldn't see. "Of course not. I'll tell you later on."

"I think you're a coincidence," he told her. "And there's nothing wrong with that. I wish you well on your journey."

"There's been no word across this table of any meaning to you," she asked, "nothing that's changed you so far?"

"'So far' is the operative term," he said. "Tell me something that shocks me, ma'am, something life-changing I can't possibly know, and I'll agree you're not coincidence."

She thought about that, a little smile. "I'll tell you something," she said. "I'm a hypnotist."

CHAPTER SEVEN

Once in a while, some word found the power to tumble Jamie Forbes and he could hear it happen, like white noise on the airplane radio when nobody's transmitting, all of a sudden the volume spikes and a rush of static in the mind.

Maybe it's thought slammed into overdrive, spun against something there's no explaining. He counted without counting . . . in seven seconds he could hear again.

How does this odd person pick my table to sit down at, the one time ever that I'm wondering did I hypnotize Maria Ochoa in the air, and remembering when it happened to me?

—The café's crowded, that's how.

How does she know what I'm thinking? She reads minds? She's somebody who looks human but maybe isn't? Why is the Unexplained happening to me here in North Platte, Nebraska some alien's got me trapped? How'd she guess my life's changing when I've never seen her before?

—Chance. Coincidence, is why. Most likely she's not from Mars.

It had been a long silence. He glanced up at the sky outside the window, then back to her eyes. "So what makes you think I think your job's going to change my life?"

The waitress arrived with breakfast. "Will there be anything else?"

He shook his head no.

"No thank you," said the hypnotist.

Alone with their toast, he looked his question at her again—why'd you think I'd care?

"I thought you'd find it interesting," she said. "I'm getting out of my own way. I'm trusting imagination instead putting it down every minute, saying it's silly. And sure enough, you're interested."

"I am," he said. "May I tell you why?"

"Please."

He told her about what had happened yesterday, sketched the story for her then this morning when

Maria told the reporter he'd hypnotized her into an airline captain, he'd been wondering if he had.

She looked at him, cool and professional. "A lot more than the airline captain, you did."

"Oh. What's hypnotism?" When Jamie Forbes was curious to learn, he didn't care if somebody thought he was stupid.

"Hypnotism," she said, as if it weren't a dumb thing to ask, "is suggestion accepted."

He waited.

She shrugged.

"That's it?"

She nodded.

"That's kind of broad, isn't it?"

"No. Tell me your story again, what you remember; I'll stop you every time you hypnotized your subject."

He looked at the clock over the lunch counter, art deco with stylized chrome propeller blades at nine and three o'clock.

"I need to be on my way."

"Have a good flight," she said. "This is important."

He blinked at the go-stop message. Maybe she's right. The weather's improving to the east, a front moving through. It's early, I can let it improve a little more.

"All right," he said, "here's what happened." He went over yesterday again, best he could recall, knowing she'd stop him come the airline part.

"First she said, *'Somebody God help me he's died!'* And I told her 'Maybe so, ma'am, but maybe not.'"

"Stop," said the hypnotist. "You suggested that she may be wrong, her husband may still be alive. That was a new thought for her; she accepted it and it gave her hope, and more than that, a reason to live."

He hadn't considered that. "I told her she could fly the airplane without him."

"Stop," said Dee Hallock. "You suggested that she could fly the airplane. Another new option."

"I said, 'We'd better get him on the ground.' I used 'we' because I thought I knew what she'd say next:"

"Stop. Not only are you hypnotizing her, you know you're doing it."

"She said, 'I can't fly an airplane,' so I said, 'OK, then you and I, we'll land it together.'"

"Stop. You're denying her suggestion that she can't fly, and your tone of voice, your confidence is affirming the opposite. Denial and affirmation—suggestions leading to a demonstration."

So it went, the woman stopping him nearly every sentence. Forbes had suggested that she had flying skills, she said; he gave her affirmation and confirmation, he used non-verbal cues, suggested she accept his authority as an instructor, suggested she could trust him to bring her down safely, confirmed suggestions with humor . . . her list went on, footnoting every sentence he remembered.

He nodded, convinced. Now this breakfast partner had him accepting her suggestion that he was guiding Maria's mind. Is hypnotism so easy?

. . . "I'm going to talk to the control tower a bit on another radio. Don't worry, I'll be listening on this radio, too. You can talk to me any time you want, OK?'"

"Stop," she said. "What are you telling her now?"

"She hardly has to do anything. Mister Authority is watching her every move, even though he's talking to somebody else."

"Exactly."

. . . "I told the tower, 'Negative, but it wouldn't hurt to roll an ambulance and a fire truck. Keep the vehicles behind the landing aircraft, will you? We don't want to distract her, equipment driving alongside when she's landing.'"

"Stop. What are you doing now?"

He smiled. "I'm hypnotizing the tower operator."

She nodded, solemn. "Yes. You are suggesting that you are in control, and that he will accept that you are."

. . . "'There's the runway ahead of us, Maria. We're going to do a big gentle turn to line up with it. Real smooth, no hurry. This is easy for you.'"

"There you have it," she said. "Suggesting a future already finished, successful."

"I was, wasn't I?"

"What do you think?" said Dee Hallock. "Telling me the story, how many suggestions, two dozen, three dozen? How many didn't you tell me about? My clients are in moderate trance after a single sentence." She lifted her teacup, didn't drink. "Suggestion-Affirmation-Confirmation, round and round, like the spirals they used to put in movies, to show someone's . . . *hyp-no-tized.* . . ."

"It isn't just me, you're saying? Anybody can hypnotize us? Everybody can do it?"

"Not only everybody *can* do it, sir, but everybody *does* it, every day. You do it, I do, all day, all night."

He guessed from her look that she thought he didn't believe.

She leaned forward, earnest. "Jamie, every time we think or say: I am . . . , I feel . . . , I want . . . , I think . . . , I know . . . , You look . . . , You can . . . , You are . . . , You can't . . . , You ought . . . , I should . . . , I will . . . , This is . . . , This isn't . . . Every time we use some value judgment: good, bad, better, evil, best, beautiful, useless, terrific, right, wrong, terrible, enchanting, magnificent, waste-of-time . . ."

Her look said you can imagine how far it goes. "On and on, every statement we make isn't a statement, it's a suggestion, and every one we accept slides us deeper. Every suggestion *intensifies itself.*"

"I tell myself I feel wonderful when I feel bad," he said, "and 'wonderful' is intensified?"

"Yes. Tell ourselves we feel wonderful when we feel bad, the badness fades with every suggestion. Tell ourselves we feel terrible when we feel bad, we get worse every word. Suggestions intensify."

She stopped, raised her eyebrows for a second. Surprised, he guessed, at her own intensity.

"That's interesting," he said, his words underlining themselves, slipping him into a trance of knowing that what she said was wildly more than interesting. If what she said were a quarter true, a tenth true . . .

"Hypnotism's no mystery, Jamie. That's all there is to it: repetition, over and over. Suggestions from everywhere, from ourselves, from every other human being we see: think this, do this, be this. Suggestions from rocks: they're solid, they're substance, even when we know that all of matter is nothing but energy, patterns of connections, which we perceive as substance. There's no such thing as solid anything, beyond seems to be."

As though she were determined not to go plunging deep again, she held her teacup, silent.

Suggestion, affirmation, he thought. The lady is right. From all the suggestions we've ever heard or seen or touched, our truth is the crowd of those we've accepted. It's not our wishes that come true, or our dreams; it's the suggestions we accept.

"You did it to Maria," she said at last, "put her so deep in trance it wasn't Maria landing the airplane, it was you. Your mind borrowing her body just long enough to save her life."

She set her teacup down as carefully as though she knew that tea must never be tilted. "Tell me this . . ." She fell silent.

"Tell you what?" he said, after a while.

"Was it possible, in your mind yesterday, that she *wouldn't* land that airplane safely?"

Silence from the pilot. Unthinkable. It was no more possible Maria couldn't land her machine than he couldn't land his own.

"When we accept our own suggestions," said his strange companion, "it's called *autohypnosis.*"

CHAPTER EIGHT

Having worn his mind on his sleeve a few years too many, Jamie Forbes had been practicing the opposite, till by now it was nearly habit.

This Dee Harmon, he thought, the hitchhiker after coincidence, has given me more to think about than she knows.

He glanced at the clock, put two ten-dollar bills on the café table. "I've got to be on my way," he said. "Anything over twenty dollars, I'm afraid you'll have to pay for it."

"Thank you," she said, "I'll do that. Where are you off to?"

"Arkansas by noon, probably. Southeast from there."

She stayed at the table as he rose. "A pleasure to meet you, Jamie Forbes," she said.

I've got to be on my way, he thought, walking from the place. I don't *got* to be at all. I could stay here and talk with this person all day, learn all she knows, a few hours worth, at least.

All right, then: I *want* to be on my way.

A suggestion which I accept, which I feel like accepting: I feel happy, leaving, walking across the ramp to the airplane, climbing again into the familiar cockpit, drying off from a flood of wild ideas, the wilder for they could be true.

Seat belt and shoulder harness buckles snapped into place, helmet on, radio cords connected, gloves on. What a pleasure, sometimes, is routine with a purpose:

Mixture—RICH

Propeller Lever—FULL INCREASE

Magnetos—BOTH

Battery—ON

Boost Pump—ON, two-three-four-five, OFF

Propeller area—CLEAR

Starter Switch—START

The propeller rotated three blades slowly, in front of the windshield, then vanished the instant the engine started, blue smoke wreathed for a second and gone in the blast.

Oil Pressure—CHECK

Alternator—ON

It had never gotten old for him, flying. Never gone boring. Every engine start was a new adventure, guiding the spirit of a lovely machine back into life; every takeoff blending his spirit with its own to do what's never been done in history, to lift away from the ground and fly.

Lifted, too, from tea and toast with Dee Holland; he gave it not another thought during takeoff.

We're flying.

Wheels up.

Airspeed and rate of climb are good. Oil pressure and temperature, manifold pressure and engine revolutions and fuel flow and hours remaining, cylinder head and exhaust gas temp in the green, fuel level's fine; check the sky clear of other aircraft, check the Earth unrolling softly below.

Once one masters the basics of flying an airplane, there's plenty of room for split personalities in the cockpit. One mind flies the airplane, the other solves mysteries for the fun of it.

Minutes later, level at 7,500 feet heading one-four-zero degrees to Arkansas, one of Jamie Forbes' minds fell to wondering why, if it were no coincidence, he had met Ms. Harrelson this morning, on her mission to prove what she's so sure is true.

Not every event needs to be labeled, he thought, coincidence or destiny. It's what happens after, that matters—whether we do something with our little life-scenes or let them slip downstream from our heart, washed to the Sea of Forgotten Encounters.

Had he hypnotized Maria into landing safely? Had he hypnotized himself that he could help her do it? Is hypnotism so common, we do it every minute of every day to ourselves and to each other and never notice?

Hypnotism doesn't pretend to tell us why we're here, he thought, but it sure chatters on about how we come to this place and how we continue playing along.

What if the hitchhiker were right, with her version, Maria landing in trance; what if it were true?

If hypnosis is nothing but suggestions accepted, then a whole lot of the world we see around us must be paintings from our own brush.

"Hello Pratt traffic, Swift 2304 Bravo's entering forty-five to a left downwind Runway Three Five Pratt." Faint on the radio, the airplane was miles away.

What suggestions? For the first time in his life, in the high noisy silence of the cockpit, he opened his eyes to see.

He flew back through time; time with himself and with others, through marriage and business, through the years in the military, through high school, grammar school, through home as a child, life as an infant. How do we become part of any culture, any form of life, save by accepting its suggestions to be our truth?

Suggestions by the thousands, millions, there's seas of suggestions; accepted, worshipped, reasonable and un, declined ignored . . . all of them pouring unseen through me, through every human being, every animal, every life-form on Earth: got to eat and sleep, feel hot and cold, pain and pleasure, got to have a heartbeat, breathe air, learn all physical laws and obey, accept suggestions that this is the only life there is or ever was or ever will be. Dee Hartridge had only been hinting.

Any statement, he thought, with which we can agree or disagree, on any level—that's a suggestion.

He blinked at that, airplane forgotten. *Any statement?* That's nearly every word he had seen spoken heard thought and dreamed, non-stop day and night continuously, for more than half a century, not counting the non-verbal suggestions to be conservative ten thousand times more.

Every split instant we perceive a wall, we reaffirm *solid-can't-go-through-that.* How many nano-instants during one day do our senses include walls? Doors? Floors? Ceilings? Windows? For how many milliseconds do we accept limits-limits-limits without even knowing we're doing it?

How many micro-instants in a day, he wondered—a trillion? That many suggestions each day in the category of architecture alone, before we move on to something simultaneously flooding suggestions about its own limits, let's say perception, biology, physiology, chemistry, aeronautics, hydrodynamics, laser physics, please insert here the list of every discipline ever conceived by humankind.

That's why infants are helpless as long as they are, even learning quicker than lightning every second. They need to accept a foundation, a critical mass of suggestions, acclimate from spirit to our customs of space and time.

Infancy is basic training for mortality. Such a savage bursting dam-break of suggestions on the poor little guys, no wonder it takes years for them to swim to the first still water, talk ideas on their own. Amazing their first word isn't "Help!" Probably is, that cry.

One hour ten minutes after takeoff, engine instruments in the green, groundspeed 150 knots in the headwind, sky clear, air smooth, ETA Arkansas an hour plus.

In the midst of all that, we mortals have to learn to be afraid, he thought. When we're mortal, danger's necessary, destruction has to be possible, if we're going to play the game.

Got to play, got to dive down deep, deep, deeper in that ocean of suggestions that we're mortal, limited, vulnerable, blind to all but the chaff-storm of what our senses tell us; turn lies to unshakable belief, no questions asked and while we're doing this avoid dying so long as possible and while we're dodging death figure out why we came here in the first place and what possible reason we might ever have had to call this game entertainment.

Oh, and all the real answers are hidden. The game is to find 'em on our own in the midst of clouds of fake answers that other players say are fine for them but which somehow don't seem to work for us at all.

Don't laugh, infant. Mortals find the game fascinating, and you will too when you accept the belief that you're one of them.

As a flying cadet, Jamie Forbes had been to classes about altitude sickness, supposed to happen when you fly high. Is there such a thing as altitude awareness, he wondered now; you understand some things, having flown some secret number of years, that you never would have known on the ground?

If you don't follow rules, you're not allowed to play.

Life in Spacetime Rule One is obvious: *You've got to believe in spacetime.*

After just a few billion suggestions about the limits of four dimensions, that is, around the time we turn two days old, confirmation comes quick. We're lost in the I Am A Helpless Human Baby trance, but we're players.

What about the ones who change their minds, who decide to withdraw their consent to this planet's sandstorm of suggestion? The ones who say, "I am spirit! I am not limited by the beliefs of this hallucinated world and I won't pretend I am!"

What happens to them is, "Poor thing: stillborn. Little tyke lived less than an hour ain't that a shame. Wasn't sick, it just didn't make it. Who said life's fair?"

The ones who go along, give their consent to be hypnotized, thought Jamie Forbes, cruising level at seven thousand five, that's us. That's me.

Groundspeed down to 135. He reset the GPS, changed his destination from Arkansas to Ponca City, Oklahoma. Never been there, he thought; will be soon.

CHAPTER NINE

"Where do you keep your books on aviation?"

The used-book store near the airport in Ponca City was promising because it had musted up in the same spot, it looked, for eighty years or so.

"What we'd have on Aviation," said the clerk, "would be, go down that way to where it says Travel and turn left. It's at the end of the aisle, right side."

"Thank you."

What they had was not a whole lot, the pilot found; nothing on his current flame, seaplane history. Three fine books, though, right together: the rare old Brimm and Bogess two-volume *Aircraft and Engine Maintenance,* way underpriced, marked three dollars each for two forty-dollar books, and Nevil Shute's *Slide Rule,* about the author's life as an aircraft engineer.

The shelf was at eye level, and when he pulled the three books together, they left a considerable hole. Normally he would have moved on, but as he was in no hurry he noticed another book in the shadows, somehow wedged behind the others. Hoping it might be *Seaplanes of the Twenties,* he pulled it forward.

No such luck. Wasn't even a flying book: Winston's *Encyclopedia of Stage Entertainers.*

Yet, struck by the title, he flashed back to Long Beach, California, the Lafayette Hotel, and looked up the only stage entertainer he'd seen in person:

> SAMUEL BLACK, AKA BLACKSMYTH THE GREAT
> American stage hypnotist (1948–1988). Through the mid-1970s, Black is said to have had no equal on the circuit.
> "What if we believed we were chained by something that doesn't exist?" he asked a *Variety* interviewer. "And what if the world around us is the perfect mirror of whatever we believe?"
> Black left the stage in 1987, at the height of his popularity.
> Journal entries recorded that he was exploring what he termed "different dimensions," and

that he had made ". . . some discoveries greatly interesting to me, and I have decided to leave my body, and return to it, while in excellent health." (*Los Angeles Times*, 22 June, 1987)

He was found dead of no apparent cause on 12 November of that year.

Black is survived by his wife Gwendolyn (b. 1951), a hypnotherapist.

Jamie Forbes set the three flying books on the bookstore counter, feeling guilty at the price on Brimm and Bogess, then handed the encyclopedia to the clerk, whom he suspected might own the place.

"This was in Aviation. It's Stage Entertainers."

"Thank you. Sorry about that, I'll restack it." He set the book aside. "That'll be three dollars each for these two, and four dollars for the Nevil Shute. Does that sound good?" As though he were willing let them go for less.

"Sounds fine. He's a terrific writer."

"*The Rainbow and the Rose, Round the Bend, Trustee from the Toolroom,*" said the clerk, with a grin at their shared good taste. "He wrote twenty-three books, you know. Everybody remembers him for *On the Beach,* but it wasn't his best book, I don't think."

He was the owner, all right.

"You know your Brimm and Bogess is way under-priced," said Jamie. "I'm taking advantage of you, that price."

The man waved his hand, dismissed the thought. "That's the way I priced it. I'll charge more next time."

They chatted for a while about Nevil Shute Norway, the writer all at once alive and with them in the book-shop, whose stories erased the distance between two folks he'd never lived to meet.

Jamie left half an hour later with the Brimm and Bogess, *Slide Rule,* and two other Nevil Shute books, paperbacks that needed rereading, and decided to stay the night in Ponca City.

Is it cheating, he wondered, to pay a store's asking price for books?

No, he decided, it isn't.

CHAPTER TEN

That evening, still happy for meeting old friends on old pages, Jamie Forbes went down for dinner in the motel restaurant.

"Welcome to Ponca City," said the waitress, with a smile that earned a lavish tip before ever she heard his order. She handed the menu and whispered a secret: "We've got great salads."

He thanked her for that, scanned down the list when she left. There was a lot to read, and the salads did look good.

"Hot chocolate and toast, I suppose."

He startled up from the page to a different smile.

"Miss Hammond!"

"Hallock," she said. "Dee Hallock. Mister Forbes, are you following me?"

Impossible. Four hundred miles from breakfast at North Platte, not in Arkansas where he said he'd be, no way for her to know, no way for him to know . . .

"You hitchhiked. To Ponca City."

"A trucker. Eighteen wheels. Three-thousand-pound pallets of North Platte sod to turn parched Ponca City green overnight. Some of the most caring, courteous people in the world. Do you know they have a Trucker's Code?"

"Come on, Ms. Hallock, this is not possible! You cannot possibly be here!"

She laughed. "Very well, I'm not here. May I join you for dinner or shall I . . . disappear?"

"Of course," he said, half rising from his place. "Forgive me. Please join me. How did you . . . ?"

"Mr. Forbes, there's no how-did-you. It's coincidence. You're not going to tell me something different, are you?"

What does one say, this happens? Does one go on in word fragments, sputtering wrecked sentences, this can't be possible this can't be happening when it's calmly happening anyway no matter what's possible?

He decided to shut up about it, but his mind tumbled, rattling on within, an empty birdcage dropped from a speeding train.

There was nothing to do but pretend this was the same world as ever, no matter how clearly it wasn't.

"She says the salads are good."

Dee laughed.

What was she thinking, the explorer of coincidences?

"Things happen for a reason," she said. "This I know. Things happen for a reason."

They ordered salads, a pasta of some kind, he didn't much care, and sat in silence. Things happen for what reason?

"I couldn't help thinking about what you said," he told her. "That suggestions hypnotize us."

"If we accept them," she said.

"When we're two days old, we don't have much choice. Much after that, it's too late."

She shook her head. "No. We always have choice. We accept because we want to accept. It's never too late to decline a suggestion. Don't you see, Jamie? It's no mystery: Suggestion, affirmation, confirmation. That's all there is to it, over and over. Suggestions from everywhere all funneled into consciousness by our own mind."

Then he decided, all this hypnotism business, to tell her something that he didn't know at all.

"Remember you said we may have a mutual friend?" he asked.

She looked up from her menu, nodded.

"We do."

She smiled anticipation. "Oh?"

"Sam Black."

No surprise, no shock, the smile changed to loving.

"You know Sam . . ." she said.

CHAPTER ELEVEN

Jamie Forbes watched her for a while, watched the face he hadn't a clue what was going on within. She just smiled that warm smile, as if, knowing Sam, he knew it all.

"How did Gwendolyn turn into Dee?" he asked. If he'd made the wrong guess about this person, that question would be crazy words.

It wasn't. "I didn't change my name when we married. But after Sam . . ." that loving smile again, ". . . died, I guess, Gwendolyn changed to Wendy, then our granddaughter, Jennifee's little girl, said it: 'Gra'ma Dee.' Everybody else agreed, while I was there."

"While you were there?"

"Her granddaughter still does, and Jennifee."

A few questions those words did raise. All of them personal, not the sort the pilot felt much comfortable asking.

"I read about him," he said.

"Stage Entertainers?"

He nodded.

"Let me guess. You found it by coincidence."

She found his story not surprising but delightful, the book squashed back behind the Aviation shelf of a used-book store in a town he never intended to land in, when he was absorbed with the question of hypnotism, on the day he met Gwendolyn Hallock Black after a lifetime not knowing she existed and hours before he was to meet her for the second time when meeting her was spectacularly impossible.

Their salads arrived, hers barely touched for his questions.

"What is it," he asked, "with you and coincidence?"

"You haven't figured that out."

"It's got something to do with hypnotism."

"You have figured that out. Do you remember my hypothesis, which you've just today helped become my theory?"

"There's no such thing." He felt like a monkey mystified by large kindergarten puzzle-pieces, dead simple to fit together, unable to make it work.

"Look at anybody meeting anybody significant in their lives, well along in the game. With your permission, may I ask . . . ?"

"Of course."

"How did you meet your wife?"

He laughed. "That's not fair! Catherine took a leave of absence from NASA, drove from Florida to California with a detour through Seattle, stopped at the little airport where I had landed after a hailstorm . . ." He halted at the edge of a long story. "You're right. It was not possible for us to meet, but it happened."

"That was . . . ?"

"Ten years ago." It had been a lovely marriage, he thought. It still is.

"I say there's no such thing as coincidence, you say there's no such thing as destiny."

"Coincidence is destiny." He said it as a joke.

She set down her fork, crossed her arms in front of her. "Do you know what you just said?"

"No coincidence," he said. "Sounds like you may not be as out-there as I thought you were."

"Remember to put it together, please," she said, no smile. "If it weren't for your miseducation, if it weren't for the suggestions you've accepted, if it weren't for your conditioned awareness by the culture you chose . . . you could walk through that wall."

He rankled at the *you*. "What about Dee? Are you miseducated?"

"I was, indeed."

"Not now?"

"No."

"You can walk through that wall?"

A smile, utter confidence. "Easy."

"Do it, please?"

"No."

"Why not?"

"You'll find out in a few hours. It's not time for you to know."

"Dee," he said. "Are you trying to frighten me?"

Instead of answering, she did a strange thing. She reached toward him, her hand open, passed it slowly from left to right in front of his face, looked into his eyes. "After this hour," she said, "you will never see me again in your life on Earth. We met, no coincidence, because it's important for you to know: *What's suggestion got to do with destiny?* The answer will change everything you believe and everything you see."

If there was anything she could have said to strike him dumb, that was it.

"She was right!" she said next minute, bright and happy, so disconnected a note it ran him off his tracks.

"Who was right?"

"The waitress! This is wonderful salad!"

"It is. A truly remarkable salad." He forgot his questions about coincidence, destiny, walking through walls, reminding anybody about anything.

She pulled a notebook from her pocket, read him *The Truckers Code*, copied from the sun visor of that Kenworth eighteen-wheeler, her ride from North Platte:

> You are the fabric that holds America together, and you are a child's best friend.
>
> It is the trucker who delivers the farmer's crops to the grocer so children don't go hungry.
>
> It is the trucker who carries the fuel that keeps them warm.
>
> It is the trucker who hauls the lumber to the carpenter to build the homes that keep them safe and secure.
>
> And it is the trucker's sacrifice of loneliness, by enduring empty nights and lonely miles, that ties America together, from the Atlantic Ocean to the Pacific.

She looked up from the notebook. "Isn't that beautiful?"

The two of them talked about that, in the restaurant in Ponca City, Oklahoma, how true the words and how much we owe the ones who choose difficult dangerous work to make our lives what they are.

Dinner was over. She wished him happy flying, then Dee Hallock said good-bye, left the table, and was gone.

In his room that evening, he set his travel computer on the hotel Internet, searched her name. There were several Gwendolyn Hallocks, of course, but only one brief mention, the one he was looking for, a fragment in some genealogy site:

> Samuel Black (1948–1988), stage hypnotist;
> m. Gwendolyn Hallock (1951–2006); daughter
> Jennifer (b. 1970).

The Internet gets numbers wrong all the time, it mangles quotes, it credits words to people who never said them, its facts are often fiction.

Once in a while, however, the Web manages to get it right. If that was so, Dee Hallock, with whom Jamie Forbes had just finished a fine salad, had died two years before they met.

CHAPTER TWELVE

It wasn't much of a sleep, that night.

That's why she could walk through the wall, he thought, thrashing sheets aside: she no longer accepts suggestions that she's mortal. *If it weren't for miseducation, you could walk through that wall.*

Is that all dying is, he thought, a dramatic change in what we believe is true about ourselves? And why do we have to die to make the change?

Because we've conditioned ourselves to believe we have to, he thought. We've married the deep suggestions of spacetime, till death do us part.

Connections like meteors: Why *shouldn't* we have to die to wake up? What suggestions do we hear otherwise?

Nobody snaps their fingers hey! we can leave spacetime whenever we want, go home when we want, come back when we want, a little vacation to get some perspective. Nobody snaps hey! we don't have to be dragged screaming out of this world by our beliefs of accident and sickness and age.

Nobody tells us dying's a custom, not a law.

He sat bolt upright in bed, two a.m.

That's what Sam Black discovered.

That's the dimension he wrote about in his journal, a dimension of *different suggestions.*

It felt like a psychic waterfall, a cascade of revelation, puzzles fitting together by themselves, the monkey watching.

That's how the man left his body in excellent health. Sam Black the hypnotist used his training to de-hypnotize himself from Conditioned Awareness, from the billions of suggestions he'd accepted, that all mortals have accepted, that we're trapped in bodies, trapped in gravity, trapped in atoms, trapped in cultures, trapped in Earth-minds so long as we play the game.

The whole sport called space-and-time, he realized, it's hypnosis! Suggestions, they're not true until we give our consent, until we accept. Suggestions that tie us are nothing but offers, proposals, until we accept and hammer them into chains, custom-made, for ourselves.

We players, we were all sitting in row A, every one of us volunteers eager for the stage.

What's in front of the audience? What's on the stage?

Nothing!

What's in front of the audience is the play of suggestions become belief become visible, ideas become stone to believers.

When it was him in that dungeon so long ago at the Lafayette Hotel, what he saw, what he battered against around him was as real as this world: tight-packed granite, cement and mortar way thick. He saw it, touched it, felt it. Hit it hard and it hurt his hand.

Yet Blacksmyth the Great walked through that wall as though it were air.

The subject believed it was rock, knew it was rock, impenetrable. The hypnotist knew it was air, nothing there to penetrate but the invisible private conviction of somebody hallucinating prison.

In the dark of Oklahoma midnight, he pressed the switch on the bedstand lamp, squinted against its light, grabbed the hotel pencil and jabbed words on the notepad.

Same as that prison, he thought, is my belief this moment, that I'm tight-packed in a body of flesh, in a motel room, sheetrock walls, keyed entry.

I never questioned my own beliefs! Long ago convinced myself and never asked again: must have air to breathe, shelter food water, see with eyes to know, hear with ears, touch with fingers. I'll see it when I believe it. No belief, no appearance.

But listen: not some simple change-my-mind-and-it'll-go-away belief, but deep every-second-of-a-lifetime convinced this game's the only truth there is.

We don't need our belief in limits to live, he wrote, *we need 'em to play the game!*

Can't play hockey without ice and stick, can't play chess without board and pieces, can't play soccer without field and goal, can't live on Earth without believing we're infinitely more limited than we are.

The pencil stopped. She's right! It's hypnotism, a hundred trillion suggestions accepted, when maybe eight would have done the trick.

So what?

Out in the night, faint, a siren. Someone's playing a fateful move, this dark moment.

So *what?* he thought.

So I don't need to get solemn, I don't need to get scared over this or that, no matter how many people believe it.

Scared over what?

Poverty, loneliness, illness, war, accident, death. They're terrorists, every one of them. And every one of them powerless the instant we choose to be unafraid.

Lamp out, head on pillow, 'round the track again.

If it weren't for the time I served in Blacksmyth's prison, he thought, this would all sound mad: a world made out of suggestions accepted, nothing's real but thinking makes it so.

Hey . . . don't assume belief's some limp-wristed half-heart. Belief has ferocious power, it's the steel vise of the game, clamps us to it every second till we die.

We die from our beliefs, he thought, every minute someone's dead of terminal illusion.

The only difference between the reality of Blacksmyth's prison and the reality of the walls around me now, he thought, is that the prison would have dissolved overnight without my dedicated reinforcement, believing. The room will take longer than that. The prison needed my personal consent to exist, this room is built from the consent of every person in spacetime: *Walls hold things in.*

Eyes closed against the dark. There is no world out there, it is every bit of it in here, he thought, suggestions become beliefs become perceptions become every so-called solid thing in our playground.

Jamie Forbes went to sleep with that.

Woke five minutes later, an attack of reason. Are you crazy, man? Thinking this stuff, the world's not really here, there's nothing out there but your imagination? Are you so susceptible to suggestion that the minute some lady comes along and says nothing's real you swallow it all one gulp?

Went back to sleep, glad that he kept his sanity.

Woke ten seconds later, what about relativity, quantum mechanics, string theory? If you think Suggestion's crazy, what about Science?

There's not just four dimensions here in spacetime, folks, because you see there's really eleven dimensions, but of course seven of them are wrapped up in little tiny balls so we don't see those. But honest, they're there!

There's holes in empty space where the gravity's so strong not even light gets out.

There's an indefinite number of alternate universes existing side by side, don't you know, a universe with every possible outcome of every possible difference that anybody could ever make in this one . . . universes with no Second

World War, universes with a Third World War that we don't know, and a Fourth and a Fifth, universes with people exactly like we are, except in about a billion of them you're called Mark instead of Jamie and you have brown eyes instead of blue.

Back to sleep again. How does it work?

Five minutes later, annoyed at himself. This is not differential calculus and me some mathophobe, he thought; this is drop-dead simple. How do we see what we see? How does a painter see the picture he paints? Here's how:

Painter look at canvas.

Dip brush into paint.

Drag wet brush on canvas.

Painter look at canvas.

Dip brush into paint.

Drag wet brush on canvas.

Painter look at canvas.

One stroke at time. Every day of our lives.

That's how it works.

Here's your paint bucket, Jamie, swirling with suggestions. Here's your brush, dip from the bucket what you'll accept for true. Here's your canvas: we call it *a lifetime*.

Now you try painting a picture, OK?

You need explanations how that works, he thought, you've got to go back long before school.

I'm hypnotized, he thought. I know how that feels, myself, personal experience, nobody has to explain. Accept suggestions and they're real, every stroke. Thirty years ago, and still I remember. There was no way I could have pounded through Blacksmyth's wall, on stage, and the wall didn't exist. I only thought it did.

Some Christian zealots on holy days, he knew, there's blood on their palms from miracle nail-wounds like Jesus' imagined in old paintings. Next Zealots Convention are you going to tell them that's not blood that's belief? Give your presentation: we've just discovered that when folks got nailed to crosses in those happy olden days they weren't nailed through the palms but through the wrists so why are you bleeding from your palms?

Answer? "Because we thought it was palms."

Are you going to tell somebody's got some illness she's dying from, tell her that's no illness that's your belief?

The thoughtful victim will say yes it's my belief and it's my belief for my own I think are pretty good reasons thank you and I intend to die from my belief, do you mind, or do you insist that I die from some different belief that you'd prefer, or at some other time that fits your schedule instead of mine?

Books with photographs for evidence—subjects hypnotized, convinced their legs are tightly bound with ropes. Minute later, day later, there's the imprint of ropes on their skin. Touched with an ice cube and told it's a hot iron, there's the blister raised at the spot. Not ropes, not irons . . . amazing powers of mind.

Not miracles, he thought, hypnosis. And not even hypnosis, that Greek mystification, but plain everyday have-a-donut?-yes-or-no suggestion, several hundred thousands of billions of times over and most answers yes. It'd be astonishing if we *didn't* see what we've been told is so!

Isn't it possible, he wondered, that this whole quantum-electric universe they say's made of tiny little strings, those strings might be created by *thought* instead of chance, atoms arranged by suggestion? And us unquestioning, lapping it up, amplifying all the joy and terror of our cultures' believings because we learn best when we're emotionally involved in the lesson we've chosen to learn and believing's the way we get there?

That's not impossible, not at all. We don't live many lifetimes, he thought, but we're free to believe we do, breath-by-breath excruciating detail. A belief in reincarnation's exactly that: a belief we experience so long as we find it interesting, useful, engaging. Disengage and the games are over.

So if suggestions build the stuff we see around us, and for all the gazillions of 'em, what really *is* a suggestion?

He puzzled that one out in the dark, fell asleep tumbling down thought-stairs.

CHAPTER THIRTEEN

Jamie Forbes woke to the motel alarm clock, dreams unremembered. Packed his bag, checked the room one last time before out the door, found a note on the stand by the bed, his own handwriting, forgotten, barely legible:

Sxggxstion = axy Contxct mxkeS us chXnge oxx Pxrceptxxns!

That's what a suggestion is, all right—whatever makes us change the way we think, and therefore what we notice. Suggestion's the flickering of some future which we can make true.

By the time he reached the airplane, he knew some contacts made him change his perceptions:

photos, paintings, movies, computers, schools, television, books, billboards, radio, Internet, instruction
manuals, meetings, phone calls, articles, questions, stories, graffiti, fairy tales, arguments, scientific papers,
trade journals, menus, contracts, business cards, lectures,
magazines, songs, slogans, poems, menus, warnings,
games, relationships, parties, newspapers, random
thoughts, advice, street signs, conversations with ourselves, with others, with animals, parties, graduation
exercises, glances, school classes, emotions, chance
meetings, coincidence,

and he poured that sea into the oceans he'd found
before.

Every event's a contact, he thought, walking around
the T-34, checking it before flying. Every one's a glitter,
noon sparkles on endless ruffled waters, each milliflash
a possibility.

He knelt to look over the left main landing gear, the
brake line, the tire. Tire's a little worn, he thought, and
realized in the daylight: that's a suggestion.

Every suggestion intensifies itself.

Tire's worn too much?

If yes: *Worn too much,*

Next suggestion: *Don't fly. Change tire.*

In order to change the tire I must find a mechanic to do the work, must locate the proper tire if it isn't in stock, stay overnight at least to change it, meet and talk with unknown number of people I wouldn't have met if it weren't for the tire, any one of whom can alter my life with a word like the hitchhiker in North Platte. My life's changing now, if I stay one day longer for the tire or three days or twenty minutes . . . new events trigger further new events, every one the result of *some sugges-tion accepted.*

Or,

If no: *Tire condition normal,*

Every suggestion intensifies itself.

Next suggestion: *Fly on as planned.*

(Trillion other suggestions in box *Do something else:* Ignored. No intensifying, no effect at all.)

But if the tire blows out next landing, it could mean big trouble.

Suggestion: *Reconsider original suggestion.*

If yes, *Time passes, weather changes, sun rises higher, coincidence patterns shift.*

If no: *Move on.*

Next suggestion: *Complete the preflight inspection.*

Ignore suggestion for now.

Accept suggestion, instead, to think about this seems-insane-maybe-isn't picture:

Every suggestion of every second, he thought, every decision we make or don't make is poised on the pinpoint of the decision that's gone before; the decision before was poised on the one before; each one elected by which suggestion I-nobody-else-I decide is true for me. No one ever makes a decision for me: when I accept advice, I'm the one chose to act on it. I could have said no, a thousand different ways.

Call suggestions "hypnosis" and all of a sudden here's a label you've been looking for, here's the pattern—the puzzle fits together. Every day, everybody in the world's going deeper into their own trance, everybody's got their own story they're believing about themselves.

My story today, he thought, is *Guy on a Journey:* Jamie Forbes flying through a cloud of decisions which leads to different changes which lead to a different life than he would have known if the left main landing gear tire had one-sixteenth inch less rubber on the tread than it happens to have this moment.

Each incident pressed alongside the one just-past just-to-come, he thought, every one a co-incident.

Seen from above, our life's this vast field of co-incidents, flowers blossoming from the decisions we've made based on suggestions we've accepted based on our belief that the appearances that surround us are true, or aren't.

The left main tire may blow out next landing; it may be good for another fifty landings, gentle ones . . . I don't need a new tire at all.

Which is what Jamie Forbes decided, that morning, kneeling by the landing gear. This tire's fine. I'll land softly. So long, different lifetimes just declined.

What's she done to me?

Never knew one airplane from another before I learned to fly. Now I do. Never noticed handwriting before I studied graphology. Now I notice. Never saw rolling cloudbursts of suggestions before Dee Hallock mentioned it's where this world comes from. *I see 'em now!*

Even what they call the Law of Attraction, he thought: "Whatever we hold in our thought comes true in our experience," that's a suggestion. Every time I try it and it works, there's a suggestion. Every time I try it and it doesn't work, there's another. When I ignore it, nothing happens . . . my life doesn't change, second by second, until the instant I do something because somehow I think it's a good idea.

Preflight finished, the pilot stowed his bag in the airplane, opened the aircraft canopy, and slid down into the cockpit.

Like everyone else on the planet, he thought, the world I see around me is my own trance vision, materialized out of whatever gazillion suggestions I've accepted along the way. Soon as I say go, it moves ahead, molasses or lightning.

So my whole world is propositions accepted, and those become beliefs become assumptions become my very own personal private executive truth.

My positive truths: "I can . . ." open the way for further suggestions, ways to go. My negatives: "I can't . . ." close the way, lodge themselves as my limit.

I'm a citizen of a psychosomatic planet, he thought. So what?

Then the pilot pressed the starter switch to START, spun the engine awake, and accepted his own suggestion: let's hold off reorganizing the universe and go flying for a while.

CHAPTER FOURTEEN

Southeast at low level over deserted land he flew, rivers and forests and wilderness, patches of old farm fields flashing below, turned to meadows.

This is what it looks like, flying in dreams, except in dreams you're not thinking where do I land when the engine quits.

So I'm a hypnotized citizen of a psychosomatic planet, he thought. So's everybody else. So what difference does it make?

That moment, for the first time, the pilot heard a new voice in his mind. Not the monkey-chatter voice that had been with him always, not his co-pilot I'll-fly-the-airplane-for-you self, not his let's-figure-this-out-together rational self; it felt like a whole brand-different mind, within, a higher self than the others.

So what? Here's what, it said. *You're the one who's hyp-notized yourself into the life you live every day.*

Here's what: You can de-hypnotize yourself.

Take all the time in the world, please, and think about what that might mean.

He touched the control stick, the sky-blue airplane lifted her nose to clear a lonely telephone wire, dropped back down over the hayfields. It feels faster today, flying 160 knots just forty feet above the ground, than it had felt going Mach 2, years ago, eight miles up. He accepted that; it was true.

Ever since Dee Hallock, why am I seeing sugges-tions everywhere?

And how would I do that; de-hypnotize myself? Slam my whole lifetime into reverse? If I've accepted, say, two or three twenty-billion suggestions that my world is just what it seems to be, what am I supposed to do now to change it?

Dying would do it. Seems to snap most people out of one trance right quick and into another. But if you . . .

. . . *WIRES!* screamed the copilot mind, *LOOK OUT! WIRES!!*

No need to scream; the pilot saw them ahead. There was all the time in the world to clear the power lines . . . the airplane lofted easily over, settled back down above the empty fields.

Much better, thank you, said the co-pilot. Careful you think about dying. Not just power lines, there's microwave towers around here, airplane-traps; remember it's not the towers that'll get you . . .

. . . it's the cables that brace the things. I know.

Stop thinking about dying, please, and look out for the wires. You want to fly low, you pay attention to the landscape, you help me out a little, here.

Jamie Forbes solved the problem with back-pressure on the control stick. In a minute the airplane cruised above the claws of most towers, slow-turning left to follow a river meandering southeast. The flying mind relaxed.

We never flew this way in the Air Force. When we lifted off some runway, we knew where we'd be landing, no matter how far away it might have been. There's no square on a military flight plan to check *we'll decide along the way.*

Not any more. Civilian flying, you take off and go, when the weather's nice. Think about landing, if you want, half an hour before you get there. Press on in the general direction; not many places in the country more than twenty minutes from a little airport.

His new higher mind didn't care for air-talk. *Want to know how you can de-hypnotize yourself?*

No, he thought.

CHAPTER FIFTEEN

Jamie Forbes landed for fuel at Pine Bluff, Arkansas, its runway afloat on a vast emerald lawn, fresh-trimmed. Nice people there, friendly to strangers as they most often are at little airports.

"Where you headed?"

"Florida."

"Long flight."

"Yes. I'm out of Seattle."

A laugh. "*Long* flight!"

Some words about the weather, a quick history of Pine Bluff flying when he asked, fuel for the airplane, then start engine once more and away.

Level at a thousand feet, instruments looking good.

Want to know how you can de-hypnotize yourself?

I never want to speak to you again, he thought. He didn't mean that, decided to be careful of his suggestions from now on, even in fun. They're powerful stuff.

OK. After I've given my consent to truck along as a mortal for a few years, how can I de-hypnotize myself without un-mortalizing myself at the same time?

You don't.

I don't understand.

Of course you understand. You do just what you said, Jamie. You un-mortalize yourself!

He laughed. This odd conversation was different from any he'd had with himself, and it was fun. Oil pressure's good, oil temp's normal.

How do I un-mortalize without dying? What's your plan?

Pretend nothing that's happened on this flight has been coincidence. Pretend it was a lesson waiting for the right time in your life to come along and that time is now.

According to what you've heard in the last twenty-four hours, how did you become a mortal in the first place?

I was hypnotized, he thought, I accepted fifty billion trillion suggestions that I'm a mortal and not pure shining spirit.

How did Sam Black bring you back from knowing you were in prison?

He snapped his fingers.

And with that reminded you who you are, that you had bought your ticket to an entertainment, that you had volunteered for the stage.

So I de-hypnotize by reminding myself . . . ?

. . . of who you were before the show began. Affirmations. Counter-hypnosis. Constant, non-stop declarations. You de-hypnotize yourself by dropping negative suggestions and affirming positive counter-suggestions.

That I'm not a mortal?

Fact is, you're not. Want to know what that feels like? Deny suggestions you're less than spirit, affirm that spirit is who you are, always have been always will be, no matter you're spirit choosing games of mortalhood.

Every player has a life beyond the game. Even you.

Interesting. He drew a pencil from his sleeve pocket, wrote the idea on the map, not far from the town of Grove Hill, Louisiana: *I'm spirit. Deny all else.*

Such as?

I don't do such-as's.

Such as . . . "I am not a limited mind, trapped in a limited body subject to disease and accident."

Nice denial. Now your affirmation, please.

He considered that. I am already spirit, here and now. Perfect. Undying.

Not bad. Shifting the definition of yourself from the trapped to the free. And you do it over and over and over, you never quit, you put down suggestions that you're mortal as fast as they come in. Every time you're aware of a hint that puts you down.

Why?

You want to know why, watch what happens when you do it.

How do I know it's true?

Hypnotized, you don't. You can't prove you're spirit. Not wanting to seem foolish, most folks accept the suggestion they're one more body killing time till time kills them.

But they're not.

There's no rush. You'll prove you're spirit when you die.

You want me to be foolish?

I don't believe in bodies, Jamie, but you do, so you'll have to tell me. How does it hurt, to identify with undestroyable spirit, instead of the vanishing beliefs of spacetime?

What a strange consciousness, he thought, this higher self. So if I'm not mortal, why did you say look out for the wires?

I didn't. That was your nicely trained co-pilot. Looking out for your belief-of-mortal-self as you were about to discover some ideas to change your life, de-hypnotizing. So long as you believe you're vulnerable to sudden dying, it warns you when it . . . LOOK OUT! TOWER!

The pilot jerked his head from the instruments, tensed to dart left-right-up-down where's the wires!!

Just kidding, said his higher self.

CHAPTER SIXTEEN

Old meadows given way to green hills and farms rolling soft below. EGT and cylinder head temperatures normal.

The LOA. You know how it works.

Not a clue, the pilot thought, enjoying this new aspect of himself. LOA. Light Observation Aircraft? Love One Another? List of Acronyms?

Law of Attraction.

Of course. Law of Attraction: whatever we hold in our thought comes true in our experience.

LOA. NYN.

What's NYN?

Now You Know.

Now I N what?

Aren't you putting things together here, Jamie? Do you think she came into your life for no reason?

He knew she came into his life for a reason, but he had more on his mind that afternoon than the mystery of Dee Hallock.

I'm running an airplane here, higher self. Maybe you could just say what's on my mind in words?

To the best of my knowledge which is pretty good, it's taking two percent of your attention to run this aircraft. You're not flying, it's flying. You're just guiding the airplane, and once it's pointed in the right direction . . .

All right, he shouted silently, I'll tell you what I know!

He didn't know what it was he knew, but the instant he began, he knew he'd find out. It had worked that way so often in his life that he trusted the odd process again, and turned it on, shifting gears, thought to words.

"What does the-world-is-suggestions-I've-accepted have to do with the Law of Attraction." he said out loud, and around the time he had said, ". . . have to do with . . ." the idea fell into place, the whole structure finished and done and true for him. Why didn't I see this a hundred years ago?

Law of Attraction: Whatever we consistently visualize, whatever we hold steady in our thought, soon or late will come true in our experience.

-plus-

Hypnotism is visualization, holding in thought: it's the Law of Attraction with a supercharger. Hypnotized, we see hear smell taste touch the suggestions we allow in our mind not sooner-or-later but right now.

An airplane, fortunately for Jamie Forbes, reacts no more instantly to thought than does the LOA, else the T-34 would have disappeared midair in a sudden explosion of understanding.

The LOA's no magic, it's no secret cosmic mystery. The Law of Attraction is hold-in-your-thought suggestions, accepted. LOA's the acronym for I'm Tranced By Every Suggestion I Accept.

The Law of Attraction, the whole thing, it's the same as, *it's the definition of hypnosis!*

More precisely, he thought, for his was sometimes a precise mind, the Law of Attraction is autosuggestion— it's self-hypnosis building stuff that, in time, other people can see for themselves.

This is only astonishing to those convinced the world is built from wood and stone and steel. It's only amazing if we've never questioned that our world is anything but what it seems to be.

Otherwise, the Law of Attraction is ho-hum of *course* all us subjects in trance are seeing visions of whatever we've agreed to see.

He swept into the landing pattern at Magee, Mississippi, enjoying the challenge of landing north in a firm west wind.

He solved it with a sideslip down final approach: the airplane banked to the left all the way down final approach, that unnatural tilt holding the machine straight despite the crosswind as the left main wheel touched the runway. Only then the right wheel touched gently down, finally the nosewheel.

He fueled the airplane, called a ride to the motel all in a whirl of understanding, a storm-trance.

He checked in, took his room key, walked past a rack of paperbacks. *Buy this book,* something suggested.

I've already got a book. The shadow of his old self, asking reasons for every smallest choice.

Buy it anyway, the blue one. He did, happily wondering why.

In his room, he pounded gently on the wall. "It is *so . . . simple!*"

Supercharged, indeed. *So this is how the world works!* He could do magic.

"Hallo Gwendolyn Hallock!" he said aloud.

He felt her smile, heard her voice in his mind: *Just keeping my promise.*

"Hallo Blacksmyth the Great!"

Have we ever seen each other, before this evening?

"Yes we have," cried the pilot softly, "Yes, Sam Black, we have!"

Open the book anywhere.

The pilot picked the paperback from where he had tossed it on the counterpane, opened it at random, eager, trusting. The words which met his eye were science, dense as black bread to the starving:

> We are focus-points of consciousness, enormously creative. When we enter the self-constructed hologrammatic arena we call spacetime, we begin at once to generate creativity particles, *imajons,* in violent continuous pyrotechnic deluge.
>
> Imajons have no charge of their own but are strongly polarized through our attitudes and by

the force of our choice and desire into clouds of
conceptons, a family of high-energy particles
which may be positive, negative, or neutral.

Attitude, choice, desire, thought Jamie Forbes. Of
course! Aware or not, conscious or not, that's what
determines which suggestions I accept. They affect
these little strings, these thought-particles this guy is
calling . . . what? He read back a sentence: *imajons.*

Some common positive conceptons are *exhil-
arons, excytons, rhapsodons, jovions.* Common
negative conceptons include *gloomons, tormen-
tons, tribulons, miserons.*

What I'm feeling right now, he thought, must be
them excytons.

Infinite numbers of conceptons are created
in nonstop eruption, a thundering cascade of
creativity pouring from every center of personal consciousness. They mushroom into
concepton clouds, which can be neutral or
strongly charged—buoyant, weightless, or
leaden, depending upon the nature of their
dominant particles.

Every nanosecond, an uncountable number of concepton clouds build to critical mass, then transform in quantum bursts to high-energy probability waves radiating at tachyon speeds through an eternal reservoir of supersaturated alternate events.

For a second the page disappeared and he saw the fireworks in his mind, movies from microscopes in orbit.

Depending on their charge and nature, the probability waves crystallize certain of these potential events to match the mental polarity of their creating consciousness into holographic appearance.

That's how I got to fly airplanes. Mental polarity. Visualizing. My own autosuggestion triggering thought-particles into . . . into what does he call them? Into *probability waves*. This guy doesn't know it, but he's describing how it works, everyday hypnotism, suggestion, the Law of Attraction!

The materialized events become that mind's experience, freighted with all the aspects of physical structure necessary to make them real and learning-ful to the creating consciousness. This autonomic process is the fountain from which springs every object and event in the theatre of spacetime.

Every object? Of course, from our consent and visu-alization. Every event? What are events but objects in proximity, acting together?

The persuasion of the imajon hypothesis lies in its capacity for personal confirmation. The hypothesis predicts that as we focus our conscious intention on the positive and life-affirming, as we fasten our thoughts on these values, we polarize masses of positive conceptons, realize beneficial probability waves, bring useful alternate events to us that otherwise would not have appeared to exist.

That's no hypothesis, he thought, it works. Sure enough, he thought. Real laws, you can prove them yourself.

The reverse is true in the production of negative events, as is the mediocre in-between. Through default or intention, unaware or by design, we not only choose but create the visible outer conditions that are most resonant to our inner state of being.

That was it. There's the so-what: We create. Our inner state of being. In what seems to be, Outside ourselves.

Nobody's passive, nobody's a bystander, nobody's a victim.

We create. Objects, events. What else is there? Lessons. Objects and events equal experiences we have, and the learning we get from them. Or don't get, in which case we create other objects and events and test ourselves again.

Was it coincidence? Of all the pages he could have turned to, in a book he felt compelled to buy, his finger came down on this one page, out of—he turned to the end of the book—400 pages. Odds 400-to-one. And this one book out of . . . how many books? Not coincidence, he thought, destiny, and the Law of Attraction at work.

That was her theory.

It's no theory, she whispered, *it's law.*

CHAPTER SEVENTEEN

Canopy cover off and stowed, next morning, Jamie Forbes slid once more into the cockpit of his airplane, mildly concerned about the weather ahead. The cold front had stalled ahead, clouds piling up over Alabama, storms with kilotons of lightning halted, thrashing in mid-air. Hardly a welcome mat for little airplanes.

Mixture—RICH
Propeller Lever—FULL INCREASE
Magneto Switch—BOTH
Battery—ON
Boost Pump—ON, two-three-four-five, OFF
Propeller Area—CLEAR

Starter Switch—START

and the welcome twisting blue-smoke thunder.

He took off watching the weather ahead on his route eastward, white clouds and some dark ones, wondering if he should have filed an instrument flight plan into what was ahead.

Instrument flight rules, though, don't allow quite the mental autopilot, the room for reflection on one's journey that visual flight rules do. He had chosen VFR, staying clear of clouds, because it was more fluid, more fun than instrument rules, which is precision flying by the numbers when you can't see outside.

Charles Lindbergh didn't have to fly charted airways from New York to Paris in 1929, he thought. Lindbergh made his own airways.

He leveled at a comfortable middle altitude, five-thousand five, smooth eagle-path S-turns around the clouds, hay-quilt farmland below, sky-quilt heaven above. Room to climb, room to glide, room to weave east between Mississippi cotton-puffs.

Somebody had to decide to become that person, he thought. It wasn't automatic welded has-to-be. Lindbergh when he started flying was the same unknown as every other student pilot in aviation. He had to decide, choice by choice, to become the man who changed the world with his airplane.

Oil pressure's good, oil temperature, fuel pressure. Exhaust gas temp, fuel flow, engine revolutions, manifold pressure.

Lindbergh had to take every step, attitude-choice-desire thousands of times over, to herd ten trillion imagons first into the likeness of five hundred dollars cash, hammer that next into the shape of a surplus Curtiss Jenny biplane, bend that into a life barnstorming, flight instructing, carrying mail, wondering, as he flew, whether the way across the Atlantic Ocean first time would be alone, in a small airplane instead of a big one.

Suggestions *you can do this,* suggestions *you can't,* he had to choose which, weed some, nourish others. When he picked *you-can,* he had to see the future in his mind (exhilaron clouds swirling, blossoming outward): a plane would need to be built, something like the M-2 mail plane from Claude Ryan, for instance, but with just one seat, all the rest not mail but *fuel* (excytons exploding)!

He must have thought it out in the air, barnstorming, his inner co-pilot flying stunts and passengers: let's say a hundred miles per hour, that'd be thirty-five hours to reach Paris; thirty-five hours flying at, say, twelve gallons per hour would be . . . four-twenty, say five hundred gallons of fuel. At six pounds per gallon, that's three thousand pounds of fuel. Have to locate the fuel on the center of gravity so the airplane stays in balance, full tanks or empty. A flying gas tank, it would have to be. It's possible, it's possible . . .

Could Lindbergh hear the hiss and crackle of conceptons over the roar of his engine?

Same time he was getting serious about the airplane, he was also gambling he might become that Charles Lindbergh lost at sea in a crazy attempt to fly a single-engine airplane, a *monoplane,* mind you, when everybody knows you need a multi-engine biplane for any such trip. To Paris on one engine—madman, that's who he was, and now there's one less Charles what's-his-name in the air.

To keep from becoming the Lindbergh of that future, the air mail pilot must have thought, my airplane will need a reliable engine, perhaps the new Wright Whirlwind . . .

Choice by choice, ideas became imajons became lines on paper became welded steel tubing covered in fabric became *Spirit of Saint Louis.*

Time to climb, Jamie Forbes decided, as the clouds stormed up into walls ahead.

Mixture full rich, propeller full increase, throttle full open. So went Jamie Forbes' day, thoughtful, and a climb to twelve-thousand five before he topped the clouds, lowered his dark-tint helmet visor against the bright.

Somebody had to decide to become the Charles Lindbergh who accepted his own suggestions, hypnotized himself to do what he wanted to do and by the way make history. The somebody who made that decision, of all the people in the world, was the guy inside Charles Lindbergh's mind.

What suggestions am I choosing to accept, Jamie thought, what have I decided to change? Who have I decided to be?

CHAPTER EIGHTEEN

Off to the south, cloud tops built up way high, twenty-five thousand feet, he guessed.

I can climb another five thousand if I have to, he thought. If there's breaks in the clouds, I can spiral down beneath cloudbase. And I can file instruments if I need to.

He'd set a backup flight plan the night before. One radio call and he could go not anywhere he pleased but "As filed," by agreement with the air traffic control center: he'd fly centerline along the airways to Marianna, Florida, through the clouds instead of around them, in case the sky got stuffed with fog.

That was Plan B. Meanwhile he cruised along at twelve-five in clear air, dodging cloud tops.

Blacksmyth the Great de-hypnotized himself right out of a body. I don't want that. I like the game too much right here; I like my life instructing, flying airplanes.

And when Sam un-mortalized himself from one consensus belief, didn't he just appear again in another, some suggestion of the Afterlife Games?

Whole new sets of opportunities, then, to accept or decline—free to believe we're spirit now, not subject to mortal limits, laws that were unbreakable an hour ago.

The convictions of others don't affect my life, he thought, until they're my convictions, too.

Soon as we're convinced we're spirit, we float through walls, invulnerable to beliefs of accident storm disease age war. We can't be buried, shot, drowned, crushed, blown up, tortured, poisoned, drugged, chained, broken, suffocated, run over, infected, trapped, lashed, electrocuted, jailed, torn, beaten, hanged, burned, guillotined, starved, operated on manipulated or messed with by any person or agency or government on Earth or galaxy or universe or law of spacetime.

Here's the downside: the minute spirits don't accept our suggestions, they can't use our playground. Drift through it, of course they can. Use it as mortals do, for schooling? Not Allowed.

What Sam did, what spirits do, is believe themselves graduated from spacetime, reflecting on the values they learned and the lessons they missed, last lifetime.

I'll make that choice when I get there, the pilot thought. For now, there's easier things to learn.

The altimeter's not real, for instance, that suggestion-of-an-instrument pointing twelve-thousand six. The altimeter's my belief in my assumptions, manifest as a disk of what looks like tin and glass, white pointers against a blackground. It isn't what it seems. It's my own imajons, polished to look like an altimeter.

The instrument's not real, not the cockpit, not the airplane, not my body, not the planet, nor the whole physical universe. Suggestions. Shifting clouds of thought-particles, following the trail of what I choose to think is so.

What *is* real?

He laughed at himself, two miles in the air. Till yesterday he was happy just to survive as a working flight instructor. Suggestions and hypnoses and particles of thought that turn the world solid as rock-particles turn stone, that was for philosophers dusting ivory towers with feather-brooms.

Now I'm thinking rock is hypnotized suggestions and wondering that if rock isn't real, what is?

What did you do to me, Blacksmyth? Things go along nice and normal for fifty years then you meet some innocent suggestion—the world isn't what you think it is—and WHOCK everything changes!

Over the nose, up ahead, he could see the clouds breaking from solid undercast to broken. Holes in the layer. Good.

That's right, he thought, everything changes. Live with it.

He eased the nose down, airspeed turning up from 185 knots to 200.

What's real is what doesn't change. Don't have to be a spaceship designer to know that; you can be a simple airplane pilot. If something was real but isn't now, then it isn't real anymore, and the question circles back, "What is real and stays real forever?"

He banked the airplane around a cloud top, rolling mist hissing by the wingtip.

Something's real. God, whatever God is. Love?

Don't need to know what's forever this minute; I'll find that out someday.

What matters now? If I don't have to de-hypnotize myself off the planet, Sam Black style, I can re-hypnotize me, instead. I can choose which trance I want to live. Long term, I can suggest myself into any heaven or hell I want to believe, right here on Earth.

Fuel state, one hour forty remaining. Clouds scattered to broken, Marianna airport's made. He trimmed the nose down, airspeed sliding up to 210.

What's that going to be, he wondered, what do I want to live? It's going to be a safe landing at the end of this flight, one more hop to home, and then . . .

And then what?

Long silence, in his mind.

Anything I want, whatever I imajon would be fun to live.

What's best, happiest?

I pretty well have it now. Great marriage, good students to teach, airplanes to fly, surviving pretty well. There's heaven enough.

So after all this change, all of a sudden I think I know how the world works, what's the change in me?

He raised his helmet visor, looked in the mirror on the canopy bow and saw himself there, not much different from this morning.

Knowing is the change. Somebody spends his life on the ground, one day he goes to flight school, comes out a licensed pilot. What's different? He can't tell, looking in a mirror, but now he has the ability to perform what he used to call miracles.

So do I, thought Jamie Forbes. So do I.

CHAPTER NINETEEN

He bought a sandwich at the Marianna airport, and a pint of milk. After the airplane was fueled, truck driven away, he sat on the ground under the wing and unwrapped the sandwich.

I know how it works. I can change whatever seems to be whenever I want to change it. What shall I change, what suggestions shall I give myself, shall I accept, take them for truth in my trance and watch the world shift around me?

He opened the Jacksonville sectional chart, colored pattern-green low elevations and empty-blue Gulf of Mexico. He took the pen from his sleeve pocket, poised it over the blue.

If I were hypnotizing me, he thought, what suggestions would I want to see come true around me? He wrote, neat printed letters, on the map:

Everything that happens around me shall work out for the good of all concerned.

People shall be as kind to me as I am to them.

Coincidence shall lead me to others who bring lessons for me to learn, and for whom I have lessons to give, as well.

I shall not lack for whatever I need to become the person I choose to be.

I shall remember that I created this world, that I can change and improve it by my own suggestion whenever I wish.

Time and again shall I see confirmation that my world is changing just as I've planned it to change, and I'll find changes better than I've imagined.

Answers to every question shall come to me in some clear way including quick and unexpected, and from within.

He lifted the pen, read what he had written. Sure enough, he thought, not a bad start. If I were my hypnotist, I'd like me to make those suggestions.

Then he did a strange thing. He closed his eyes and imagined an advanced spirit there with him that moment, under the wing of the airplane.

"Is there anything," he whispered, "you'd care to add?"

As though the pen had come to life in his hand and was writing by itself, in larger, bolder strokes than his own:

I am a perfect expression of perfect Life, here and now.

Every day I am learning more of my true nature and of the power I've been given over the world of appearances.

I am deeply grateful, on my journey, for the parenting and guidance of my highest self.

Then it was still. While the pen moved, he felt as though he were standing in a science museum close by some giant van de Graaf generator, electrics coursing through his body, his hair tingling. When the words stopped, the energy faded.

Whoa, he thought, what was that? He laughed at himself. That's the answer to, Is there anything you'd care to add?

Unaware, for it was deep in his subconscious, the response: *Answers exist before you ask your question. If slow is necessary, please make that clear in your request.*

He unfolded from under the wing, the world feeling not quite the same as it had a minute ago. He did not catch the significance of the strange word *parenting*, he did not remember to thank whoever it was that had done the writing.

CHAPTER TWENTY

Airborne southbound from Marianna, the afternoon thunderstorms were lighting off in earnest. His airborne GPS showed tops to 42,000 feet, pools of crimson warnings splashed along the course ahead.

Jamie Forbes forgot about suggestions for a while. Hypnotized or not, when flying small airplanes one doesn't mess with thunderstorms, and the monsters had his attention.

Unable to climb high enough to clear the tops, he chose a thousand feet for his altitude, moving fast, the little airplane weaving between dark columns of rain.

Heavy drops spattered then pounded the aircraft, pressure-washing wings and windshield clean and bright while he turned back toward clear air.

No instrument flying today, he thought. It's a fine little GPS, but fly on instruments near thunderstorms, let the display screen pick this time to go dark . . . that would not be fun.

Why is it that airplane instruments almost never fail on nice days when you don't need them? It isn't that you can count on 'em to fail when the weather's awful, just that it happens often enough that you want to be ready, you've got to have backups.

He was running low on backups, just now. This far along, wide forests of scrub pine below, the way back to Marianna closed in curtains of silver chainmail from the clouds. Not all of it violent, but here and there visibility down to a mile—legal to fly but not safe in a fast airplane.

He reached the map from the floor, found his position. Nearest airport six miles southwest. He looked that direction, saw the place smothered in buckshot rain.

Having tried landing in the middle of a thunderstorm as a young pilot, he had declined the suggestion ever to try again.

Next nearest airport is Cross City, fifteen miles southeast, sky broken to overcast, thunderstorm closing from the west. He turned that direction, having abandoned his straight-line course for zigzags from airport to airport, a frog on lily pads.

When all the airports ahead go down in storms, he had decided, I'll land at the last one open, wait on the ground till the wild moves on. That time would be now.

Ten miles from Cross City he saw the storm, approximately as black as midnight. *You'll make it if you're fast.*

He pushed the engine to full power, lowered the nose and the little airplane leaped ahead, airspeed winding toward 190.

He said it aloud in the cockpit, unsmiling: "My highest self is cutting this one a little fine . . ."

Eighty seconds later he saw the runways at Cross City, a wall of water like a thousand-foot tidal wave thundering in from the west. Beneath it, lightning glittered and forked in the dark.

"Cross City traffic, Beech Three Four Charlie is one mile northeast initial for a three-sixty overhead Runway Two One Cross City traffic permitting."

Traffic permitting. As if there'd be any traffic landing just now. Somebody'd have to be crazy, to be in the pattern with the storm seconds from strike.

Uh-oh, he thought, *that's me!*

The '34 flashed down the runway a hundred feet up flying just this side of 200 knots.

Throttle to idle, pitch up and turn to downwind, airspeed falling with the climb, gear handle Down, flap lever Down, dump the nose and steep turn to final, the end of the runway whirling softly up to meet him, going gray in rain. A few seconds after Wheels-Down showed in the landing gear position indicators, tires splashed on wet pavement.

One minute later, taxiing to the parking ramp, Jamie Forbes became a goldfish in an air-bowl, cloudburst roaring torrents on the canopy so he couldn't tell the engine was running except the propeller still turned. Farther than that he couldn't see.

He braked to stop on the taxiway, deluge roaring unchecked, carefully folded his map as lightning bolted near, thunder jolting the airplane on its wheels.

At the edge of the chart, in bold letters:

I am deeply grateful, on my journey, for the parenting and guidance of my highest self.

Safe in the midst of violence was the first he noticed *parenting.*

CHAPTER TWENTY-ONE

Thanks to the Southeast Horseperson's Convention in Gainesville, every motel in Cross City was sold out. Each clerk was polite *(People shall be as kind to me as I am to them)*, each told him there was no room, no suite, no broom closet, no doghouse available till Monday.

He decided that he'd unroll his survival blanket under the wing tonight, pray for dry, and press on south in the morning.

The dry didn't quite materialize, but the mosquitoes did. Not long after dark, they had hummed him from any idea of sleeping under the wing. He retreated to the cockpit, shut the canopy tight against the little beasts, stretched as much as he could by angling against the left side of the seat back, crowding both feet in the right rudder-pedal well.

He improved his time by reading the T-34 Pilot's Handbook yet again, by flashlight, 151 pages of absorbing text and photos. He managed thirty-three of them before the batteries dimmed and died.

Alone, cramped, hot, wet, dark; ten more hours till dawn. Is this what you get when you accept suggestions to change the world around you?

You didn't suggest a comfortable bed every night, something said. You suggested a different world, one that you'd imagine true. You have it. If what you meant was no challenge, you should have said so. If what you meant was no discomfort, you should have made a note of that.

He considered finding the spare flashlight batteries and adding I Shall Have No Discomfort to the list of suggestions. Alone and hot, cramped and wet and beginning to suffocate in the closed cockpit, he smiled as he thought about changing his list of autohypnotic suggestions.

I Shall Always Have Plenty of Fine Food to Eat, And Oh by the Way I Shall Sleep Late Every Morning and Never Have to Take the Trash Out or Pay Bills.

Someone camped not far away about then, listening in the dark, would have heard him laugh.

CHAPTER TWENTY-TWO

He nearly remembered the dream, not quite. The last hour before sunrise, the pilot had fallen asleep. He had been back in school, or back at least in a place surrounded by empty blackboards.

There had been thousands of words on the boards, but all of them erased, rows on rows of chalk-film eraser-marks. Then came one board, just before he woke, with one word, not chalked but chiseled in stone:

Life

There was a half-second to see it before the blackboards spun away and he woke to first light east, clear dark skies.

A man who didn't remember dreams, Jamie Forbes grabbed the last fragment, held till it dissolved in the dawn.

The dream's my answer, he thought. At last!

Now, holding the answer, he went looking for the question. Life, he thought, life-life-life. Shall I write it down? Seemed silly, but the map lay on the right switch-panel console. He pulled his sleeve pen and wrote it: Life.

It had seemed so important to remember that. Minute by minute, it was looking sillier. Life. Okay. Seconds ticked. Okay became Now-what became So-what. Life. Nice word, but it could use a little context.

He climbed from the cockpit into cool air, mosquito-free, pretzel determined to be bread-stick. From the wing to the ground was a two-foot jump, felt like four.

Wuff, what a night. I am stiff, stiff, stiff!

There in the sunrise, before he took the chains for true . . . : No! I will NOT repeat after you! I reject your dull suggestion about my feelings I shall not trance myself sick or limited or unhappy. I am not stiff stiff stiff, I'm the opposite. I am a perfect expression of perfect Life, here and now. I'm limber as a snake, this morning. I feel zero pain, zero discomfort. I am in perfect health, full of energy, sharp, alert, rested and ready to fly!

At one level he knew he was playing at his de-hypnotizing trick, at another he wondered if it might work.

To his startlement, it did. Stiffness disappeared, vanished in the first half of the first second he pushed the suggestion away instead of hugging it, some blood-sucking vampire pal, to his neck.

He practiced walking, in the predawn, as though he were perfectly un-stiff, and like some miraculous Bible healing he walked easily, relaxed and normal.

Applause, from an inner gallery. It was a miraculous demonstration, by reflex: near-instant denial of negative suggestion, affirmation of real nature, suggestion vanished into rejection-limbo, ability-to-walk restored in seconds.

This world, it really isn't what it seems, he thought, jogging now along the dim taxiway, tasting victory. Since it's going to be suggestions one way or the other, why not take the bright ones for true, instead of the drags? Is there something wrong with that?

I'll look at it this way: I'm rewiring myself. Every time, I'll swap the negative energies for the positive, and see what happens. God knows I've bought the downs long enough in this lifetime, now it's the ups' turn.

Feels strange, that such a simple thing as— He interrupted at once. Doesn't feel strange at all! Feels natural, normal; feels right!

He smiled at himself. Let's not get carried away . . . No! I'm already carried away, with my rewiring. It works! Only stuff gets through my gates is positive life-affirmers!

I reserve the right to refuse negative suggestions from anyone.

Come on, growled this feisty new optimist within him to the forces of darkness, what's your next put-down for me? Roll 'er out. Take your best shot!

Jamie Forbes laughed at the battle for his mind, put his money on the new guy there.

Thank you, he thought to the teacher within. I expect you're gonna see big changes, starting now.

CHAPTER TWENTY-THREE

After the storms, the sky had gone wide open. Severe clear, as pilots say, the whole southeast.

Expect little puffs of cumulus around noon, thought Jamie Forbes, preflighting his airplane. Puffs building to thunderstorms again by mid-afternoon.

By the time the sun had cleared the horizon east, the T-34 was wheels-up and climbing, southbound. Air cool and smooth as buttered ice. He visualized his landing at home, a perfect touchdown, taxiing to the hangar.

Level at three-thousand five, an impish part of his mind became advocate of the devil; he pushed it onstage.

May not be a perfect landing. Something could go wrong. Engine could quit. Complete electrical failure. Wheels might come halfway down and jam.

He waited for the attack of his inner optimist on these dark ideas, denying them all. Nothing happened.

Oil line could break.

It could.

Aren't you going to say Impossible? No Negatives Allowed?

What's negative about an engine failure? Part of the reason you like flying is the unexpected. Oil line break is an event, a test. No more negative than a spelling test.

Of course. You're right.

You want to know negative, Jamie? Here's negative:

"I'm sick."

"I'm trapped."

"I'm dumb."

"I'm scared."

"I'm separated from my highest self."

Negative is not the test, negative is what you get when you fail it.

Why not No Tests, replied the pilot, hypnotize my appearances into trouble-free flying?

Nope don't you want to know why.

Why?

Because you love passing tests, you love proving yourself.
The pilot considered that. Not just airplane tests.
Not just airplanes. All tests.
Why are you so confident, when I'm not?
Since you just bought a suggestion that you're not, I'll tell you why. I'm confident because I don't wonder if what I see around me are my own beliefs. I know they are. I know I bring them to me for important reasons. With your permission, I'll fill the Confident square for a bit, till you're comfortable doing it on your own.
Thank you, but . . .
But what? Are you planning to put a negative in that blank?
The pilot was not known for being slow of mind. He dropped " . . . I'll never be able to do this all the time" like a hot turkey.
Thank you, but . . . I don't need your help.
He sensed amusement from his higher self.
Good. Let me know if ever you do. 'Bye.
It felt a little lonely, his new friend gone.
"It does not feel lonely!" he said aloud. Not gone at all, but just met. Finding selves in high places, that feels fine, and they answer when I call.
The confidence he pretended flared into confidence he felt, his second instant healing of the day. Something

had changed within Jamie Forbes. All this talk of Hypnotism by Culture was no empty play of words. The more he examined the idea the more he saw for himself it was true.

Answers to every question shall come to me in some clear way, including quick and unexpected, and from within.

The airplane slanted up through the top of the haze layer at four-thousand five, whisking by popcorn clouds dreaming giant futures. For a second its shadow fell on a layer of white mist, airplane silhouette in sharp black light, centered in a halo of technicolor rainbow, full-circle round.

Oh, my, the pilot thought. Flying airplanes, you get eye-pictures like this, half-second snapshots you carry forever. What a life!

The word on the blackboard, he remembered; isn't that interesting, the word from his dream. He puzzled a bit, why *Life* solitary, all others erased?

Do we have to tell you?

Hello again.

You wanted to know what's real, remember?

Since everything else is suggestions and appearances, yes, I did. Oh. Life? *Life's* real?

Level at five-thousand five, his thought-form propeller lever eased back toward Decrease, dropping the belief of revolutions from 2,700 per minute back to 2,400 on the not-there tachometer. Can't trust vision or hearing or touch to teach me Real, they're all part of my trance.

Yet I know, that I live. That's real. *I am.*

Have ever been, came the whisper. *Shall ever be.*

For all the fakery in now-you-see-it-now-you-don't spacetime, he thought, for all its suggestions and misdirections, its assumptions and beliefs, for all its theories and laws and pretending we're somebody we're not, namely erect-walkers on the cooling surface of spherical melted stone, one of a dozen planets drawing forever-spirals about a continuous nuclear explosion in a pinwheel galaxy in a fireworks universe; behind our mask, it's *Life* that's the never-born never-dying infinite eternal principle, and the real me is one not with dying fires but with *It!*

Us on our little belief of a home; ancient aliens in their belief of star-flung civilizations; spirit-creatures from beliefs of afterlives and dreams of dimensions beyond; inside we're all playing at symbols, we're each of us the spark and flash of undying Real.

He blinked at himself. What's this I'm thinking? How do I know this stuff?

It's because you fly airplanes, Jamie . . .

Oh, come on! That can't . . .

. . . and because like everybody, it's already within; you've known it all along. You're just deciding to remember, along about now.

Is it fun for you?

Creating worlds? It's fun, all right, doing it well. As you . . . as we all find out when we realize it's worlds we're creating, every suggestion, image, statement, affirmation . . .

I'm going to find out?

There's no going back, unless you're desperate for boredom.

The pilot balanced on the edge of what he'd been waiting a lifetime to learn.

Let me get this straight, he thought, tell me if I'm pointed in the right direction. We're floating around somewhere, we imagine a story that would be fun to live . . .

We're not "floating around somewhere." Where'd you get that?

. . . we imagine our story, and so imagine ourselves into players who can act that story.

We don't need to be in any story, said his other self. *But . . . OK for now. Go on.*

We create ourselves out of imagination, suggestions and ideas; we attract ourselves into an environment where lots of folks are in the kind of trance we want to be in.

I shall remember that I created this world, that I can change and improve it by my own suggestion whenever I wish.

We can steer our story any direction any time, but our belief in spacetime is our sea, it's our stage, and soon as we forget we can change it, we live an uncreative trance instead of a creative one.

"Creative trance." That's very nice.

We don't *have* bodies, we continuously imagine them. We become that which we constantly suggest to ourselves, sick or healthy, happy or hopeless, thoughtless or brilliant.

He stopped, waited for feedback. Silence. Hello?

I'm listening. Go on.

That's about it. That's where I am right about now.

That isn't where you are. You're way beyond that. But that's where you believe you are, and that's fine. Am I reading you right, dear mortal? You've just discovered your blue-feather wings; you've always had 'em inside, living your fantasy of flight. You're standing on a cliff a mile high, you're leaning forward, trusting, wings out, you're this minute losing your balance on the ground, hoping you'll find it in the air?

Yes! Finding my balance in the air!

Nice.

That was the last word Jamie Forbes heard from his higher self for a while. He spent that time listening to what he had just said, himself.

CHAPTER TWENTY-FOUR

By the time the first raindrop of the first storm of the afternoon touched the ground, the T-34 was landed, fueled, rolled safely into its hangar. The pilot drove home in the rain, let flying go, savoring time ahead with Catherine, at last. So much to tell her, so much he wanted to hear what she'd say.

He took the next day to remember what had happened on this trip, relived the flying, relived the listening and the ideas, put it down as much as he could, word for word. It came to seventy pages in the computer.

His students waited, patient as condors.

"What would you do," he asked, next training flight in the little Cessna with Paolo Castelli, "if the rudder jammed?"

"I'd steer with the ailerons."

"Show me."

Then, "What would you do if the ailerons jammed?"

"So now the rudder and the ailerons are jammed, sir, or just the ailerons?"

"Both jammed. I'll freeze up on rudder and ailerons now, you can't use them."

Long silence. "That can't happen."

"Happened to me," said the instructor. "Toolkit slid under the rudder pedals, sleeve of a little girl's jacket got pulled into an aileron cable pulley. That's how I learned what you're learning right now."

"I don't know."

"Doors, Paolo. Open the doors and watch what happens."

The student unlatched the door, pushed against the torrent of wind outside.

"Man! It turns the airplane!"

"Sure enough. Give me a ninety-degree turn left, then one to the right. Doors only."

Near the end of the lesson, the question had grown: "What would you do if the rudder jammed, and the ailerons and the elevator, and the trim cable broke, and all the instruments failed and all the radios, and the throttle stuck full open, maximum takeoff power?"

"I'd . . . I'd use the doors, and the mixture control to shut the engine on and off . . ."

"Show me."

It was hard work for his students, these chapters of their training, but instead of scared they flew away confident, after his lessons, came back for more.

At two thousand feet, he pulled the throttle back to idle. "Miss Cavett, that engine has quit yet again! Where will you land?"

The student relaxed for the fifth forced-landing practice of the flight. All routine: instructor pulls the power, student finds a field, glides into a landing pattern as though it were a runway. When her instructor sees that she'd make a safe landing, he advances power, airplane climbs back up to altitude.

But this time was different.

"That's where you're going to land?"

"Yes, sir," she said. "The brown field, next to the dirt road."

"You'll land crosswind, across the rows?"

"No. Into the wind, with the rows."

"You're sure you can make it?"

"Yes, sir. I'll make it, easy."

Jamie Forbes pulled the mixture control to CUT-OFF. The engine dropped from idle RPM to zero, the propeller shuddered to a stop, soft hushing silence of the wind, airplane become glider.

"Excuse me, sir, did you just . . ."

"Yes. Give me your best full stop landing, Miss Cavett, into your field."

Jamie Forbes had thought that he specialized in flight instruction that pilots can't find, this side of their first emergency in the air. Now he knew it was something different.

I don't teach, he realized. I suggest, and the students teach themselves.

I offer ideas. Why not try opening the doors? Why not try flying by feel instead of instruments? Why not try landing in that hayfield full stop, then get out of the airplane and jump up and down in the hay, prove to yourself that bare ground's as good as any runway when you have to land?

Who said it? "You're not an instructor, you're a hypnotist!"

Maria! Flicker of a second, he was in the air over Wyoming.

*I'm going to die and he's asking me about **cake?** Of all rescuers I get a **crazy-man?***

It was Maria Ochoa, she who took coincidence to save her life and touch mine, showed me how the world of spacetime works. Hypnotizing Maria was not some twenty-minute help I gave her, it was a gift she gave, to change me forever.

Dear Maria, he thought, wherever you may be right now, I shall pass your gift along.

Once in a while he'd get a letter, a call, an e-mail from a student, "So when the engine stopped—well, while the engine was blowing up—I got the fuel off, the mixture off, prop full decrease, I heard your voice right beside me: *Give me your best full-stop landing to your cow-pasture, Mister Blaine.* There was oil all over the windshield, Mr. Forbes, but I stood on the rudder, slipped the turn to final so I could see out the quarter-window all the way to flare. Not a scratch! Smoothest landing I ever made! Thank you!"

He kept the letters.

I am deeply grateful, on my journey, for the parenting and guidance of my highest self.

It was a grey morning, ceiling zero visibility zero in fog. He was sitting at his computer, writing a check for the hangar rent *(I shall not lack for whatever I need to become the person I choose to be)* when the telephone rang.

"Hi," he said.

A woman's voice, a little nervous, on the phone. "I . . . I'm calling for Jamie Forbes."

"And you have found him."

"Are you the flight instructor?"

"I'm a flight instructor. I don't advertise, though. You called an unlisted number."

"I want to learn to fly. Can you teach me?"

"I'm sorry, ma'am," he said, "I'm not that kind of teacher. How'd you find this number?"

"On the back of a flying magazine. Somebody with a marker pen wrote your name and the number and 'Good instructor.'"

"That's nice to hear. I teach the sort of things you want to know after you've got your license, though. Seaplanes, tailwheel aircraft, advanced flying. There's plenty of flight schools around, and if you want some extra training, later on, give me a call and we'll talk about it."

"Don't hang up!"

"I was planning to wait," he said, "till you said good-bye."

"I'm a good student. I've been studying."

"That makes a difference," he said. "What's a sideslip?"

"It's a maneuver . . . that seems odd, at first," she answered, glad for the test. "You bank the airplane in one direction, but yaw it in the other. A sideslip keeps you from drifting in the wind when you're landing, it's the only way to go straight in a wind that would blow you off the runway."

"Nice definition." He had expected the textbook: "a way of losing altitude without gaining airspeed," which is only partly true.

"I've always wanted to fly. So did my mother. We were going to learn together, but she died before . . . before we did."

"I'm sorry to hear that." It would have been fun for them, he thought, learning together.

"I talked to . . . I dreamed about my mom, last night. She said I can learn for us both, she'll be flying with me. Then this morning I found this magazine in a grocery cart with your number on it. It's as if . . . I know you teach *some* first-time students, don't you? Almost never?

Careful interview? Those who have to learn for two, they study twice as hard?"

He smiled, at that. It wouldn't be the end of the world, he thought. She's got the right attitude, for sure. *Attitude, choice, desire to make it true.*

They talked for a minute, set a time to meet.

"Mom said you choose your flight instructor by the color of his hair," she said, relaxed now, happy. "I know I'm being silly, but you do have gray hair, don't you?"

"In all modesty," he said, "I do. And by the way, if you don't mind my asking, what's your name?"

"I'm sorry," she said, "I guess I got a little carried away, there. I'm Jennifer Black O'Hara. My friends call me Jennifee."

When the call was finished, plus seven seconds till the shock of her name no longer paralyzed, he wrote it, neat shaky letters, in his flight schedule.

Coincidence shall lead me to others who bring lessons for me to learn, and for whom I have lessons to give, as well.

He didn't mention it to her, but he thought it likely that the hypnotist's daughter would pass her interview and learn to fly. That they'd pass it together—Jennifee and her mother, both.

—END—

Hampton Roads Publishing Company

. . . for the evolving human spirit

HAMPTON ROADS PUBLISHING COMPANY
publishes books on a variety of subjects,
including spirituality, health, and other
related topics.

For a copy of our latest trade catalog,
call 434-296-2772,
or send your name and address to:

HAMPTON ROADS PUBLISHING COMPANY, INC.
PO BOX 8107 • CHARLOTTESVILLE, VA 22906
E-mail: hrpc@hrpub.com • www.hrpub.com